Unexpectedly
EVER AFTER

THE
oops baby
CLUB

HEATHER ASHLEY

Copyright © 2025 by Heather Ashley

All rights reserved.

No part of this book may be reproduced in any form or by any electronic or mechanical means, including information storage and retrieval systems, without written permission from the author, except for the use of brief quotations in a book review.

ISBN # 9798280927162

heatherashleywrites.com

For everyone who needs an escape from the shitshow of life right now.

At least we still have orgasms.

PLAYLIST

"Fire Meet Gasoline" by Sia
"Walls" by Kings of Leon
"Can't Help Falling in Love" by Haley Reinhart
"Home" by Phillip Phillips
"Control" by Halsey
"Burn" by Ellie Goulding
"The Middle" by Zedd & Maren Morris
"Stubborn Love" by The Lumineers
"House of Gold" by Twenty One Pilots
"Flaws" by Bastille
"Run Into You" by Clara Mae
"Coming Home" by Leon Bridges
"Better Together" by Jack Johnson
"Freckles" by Natasha Bedingfield
"Turning Page" by Sleeping At Last
"Bloom" by The Paper Kites
"Everything Has Changed" by Taylor Swift ft. Ed Sheeran
"Stand By You" by Rachel Platten
"For Once in My Life" by Stevie Wonder
"Accidentally In Love" by Counting Crows

1
Clover

I'VE NEVER UNDERSTOOD people who can't keep their shit together.

"Vodka soda, two whiskey neats, and a margarita with no salt," I repeat back to Mr. Wall Street with his watch that costs more than an entire year of my student loans and his eyes that never quite reach my face. It's because they're on my boobs, but I like to think he's got a small dick and this is the most action he'll get this month.

See? Keeping my shit together. Snapping at the guy's only going to mean losing out on tip money, I need more than my dignity.

He barely nods before turning back to his friends, but I couldn't care less. The less interaction, the better.

Friday nights at Ember are always pure chaos. I can't mix cocktails fast enough, and despite the upscale vibe of our trendy Portland bar, these suited professionals turn into animals after their third-ish drink. My hands fly over bottles and shakers and glasses and ice so fast, I don't even have time to think. Good thing all I need is muscle memory.

My fingers are sweaty, and the margarita glass slips in my

grip. I grit my teeth and flex my fingers to hold on. They ache, but I save the potential disaster at the last second. I'm tired as hell, and not as sharp as I should be after the double shifts I've pulled all week. But I'll rest when I'm dead. There's no time for weakness or sleep when you've got goals as big as mine.

"Your eye's doing that twitchy thing again," Navy says as she slides past me behind the bar, her electric blue hair tips catching in the light. "The one that only happens when you're in your 'I'm running on fumes and spite' era."

I touch the corner of my eye reflexively. Yep, it's totally twitching. "It is not."

"You know I have eyes, right?" She grabs three bottles of tequila without looking, her movements so graceful it's annoying. "When's the last time you had fun? And making to-do lists doesn't count."

"Wednesday." I lean forward to deliver drinks to Wall Street and flash him my pay-my-rent smile. He adds an extra five to the tab, his eyes dropping momentarily to my not-at-all-sluttily-displayed cleavage before I straighten up. What can I say? The system works. "I alphabetized my spice rack by region and cuisine. You have no idea how satisfying that was."

Navy's laugh follows me down the bar. "God, you're hopeless. You need to get laid before your vagina seals shut."

"No, what I need is to pass Business Analytics," I counter, already mixing a Manhattan for a woman in a killer dress who's been waiting with the patience of someone who knows what it's like on this side of the bar. "My final project is due Monday. I have quarterly projections with Theo tomorrow, and somewhere in all of that, I need to do laundry because I'm officially down to my emergency underwear."

"Emergency underwear?" Navy perks up. "Please tell me it's something slinky and black you've been saving for a special occasion. Like..." She taps her black tipped finger against her lips as she pours a draft beer one-handed. "Getting railed in the bathroom at work by one of these random suits."

I snort. "It's the five-pack of ugly briefs I got at Target because I keep putting off laundry day." I slide the Manhattan across the bar with a genuine smile. The woman winks at me and I sigh. She's who I want to be when I grow up. Someone with tons of confidence who knows exactly what she's worth. People don't walk away from a woman like that.

For the next three hours, it's just me and the booze and the neckline of my tank top getting progressively lower and lower as people get drunker and looser with their wallets. *C'mon, douchebags. Give up your money. Mama needs to open her bar.*

I pour, shake, and serve on repeat until my brain feels like it's been through a blender. My mental to-do list scrolls on a loop while I try to figure out a plan for how I'm going to get it all done over the next forty-eight hours: four-hour study sesh minimum (kill me now) to prep for my final, tackle laundry mountain, go on a journey to the grocery store (this is literally what it feels like to me, a whole-ass epic quest), do enough meal prep so I don't die of starvation this coming week, and of course, the inventory spreadsheet, which might be the only thing I'm actually looking forward to. Maybe if I skip breakfast tomorrow (because who needs food?), I can cram in another hour of Business Analytics before my meeting with my boss.

By the time the last stumbling, slurring mess of a human finally clears out, my feet feel like they're bleeding. I must look about eighty with the way I'm hobbling around while I close out the register.

We crushed our previous Friday night record, and despite how exhausted I am, I get a little rush knowing it was the changes I've implemented that did it. That quarterly bonus might just be enough to toss another sad little crumb into the gaping maw of my "Clover's Bar" fund. Five years of this grind, and I'm still just inching my way to freedom, but goddammit, I *will* make it happen.

"Alright, that's it. Operation: Get Clover Laid and Slightly Less Stressed is a go." Navy leans against the sticky, liquor-soaked back bar, already changed into her non-work clothes in skin-tight jeans and a crop top that barely contains her awesome octopus tattoo—those tentacles look like they're climbing up and down her torso and I'm kinda jealous she was brave enough to get it. "We're going dancing. Right now."

"Are you high?" I keep wrestling with the mountain of cash from the register and the pile of rubber bands beside it, not even glancing up at her insane suggestion. "Some of us have actual adulting to do and can't afford to be hungover or sleep until two tomorrow."

"All of us have responsibilities. Some of us just remember we're twenty-six, not dead." Navy yanks the elastic from my messy bun, and my dyed-black hair tumbles down around my shoulders, suddenly making me feel even grungier. When did I last wash my hair? Three days ago? Four? Shit, I can't remember. "Live a little, Clover. The world won't spontaneously combust if you have fun for one damn night."

"My Business Analytics grade might." I swat her hand away, wincing as a sharp pain shoots through my aching wrist. "Besides, I look like I rolled around out back behind the dumpster. I'm sweaty and gross."

"You look like a hardworking bartender who deserves tequila and some no-strings-attached fun to work out those kinks. Besides, you'll only get sweatier when you dance, so no one will notice." Her eyebrows do a suggestive wiggle. "Lucky for you, tequila's the first step and pretty soon you won't care about the rest."

The bell above the front door chimes, and my automatic "We're closed" is already forming on my lips. But the words die before they can escape when I see Kasen's broad frame filling the doorway, his expression tight and unreadable. My stomach plummets faster than the stock market during a crash.

"Kasen?" My brother *never* shows up here at this ungodly hour, at least not without us having plans. He's got a look on his face I don't like. That's his "someone's in the hospital" or "the brewery's on fire" look. "What's wrong?"

"Nothing's wrong." He tugs on his favorite black beanie, a nervous habit he's had since we were kids. "Can't a guy just drop by to see his favorite sister?"

"I'm your *only* sister, Kasen, and you're so full of shit your eyes are turning brown." I narrow my eyes at him, already bracing for bad news. "You've got *that* look."

"What look?"

"The same look you had when you shattered Mom's favorite vase playing indoor baseball and tried to convince her the house was haunted and a ghost did it."

Navy snorts a laugh. "Alright, well, this is my cue to make like a tree and get the hell out of here." She grabs her jacket and keys. "Text me tomorrow, Clover. Or don't, if you're actually out doing something I would do. Bye Kase!"

Kasen waves at my bestie and then waits until Navy's out the door before sliding onto a barstool. "I need whiskey. The really good stuff."

Now my gut is officially twisting into knots. Kasen owns Timber, the brewery two blocks over. The guy's such a craft beer fanatic he practically breaks out in hives if someone even mentions Bud Light in his presence.

"Spill it, dude." I pour a generous two fingers of Macallan neat and slide it across the sticky countertop to him. I frown at it. I need to remember to wipe it down before I take off. "Whatever it is can't be as bad as that time you tried to brew that weird raspberry beer in your bathtub and flooded the entire floor."

He downs half the scotch in one gulp, then makes a face

like he just swallowed battery acid. He's *so* not a liquor guy and I laugh at the face he makes until his next words sober me right up. "I need a favor."

"Okay..." I draw out the word, shifting my weight onto one hip, my feet still throbbing.

"A friend of mine needs a place to crash for a couple of months."

"A couple *months*?" My eyebrows shoot up.

He avoids my gaze, fiddling with the edge of his beanie. "Three, tops."

The knot in my stomach actually loosens a little, and a laugh bubbles up. "That's it? Seriously? I was expecting you to tell me you accidentally stole someone's baby or something. I can ask around at the bar—"

"No, I mean with you. At your place."

I blink, feeling like I've suddenly missed a crucial plot point. "My shoebox apartment? The one where I can stand in the middle and almost touch both walls? *That* place?"

"It's bigger than those glorified closets they call studios," he argues, finally meeting my eyes, a hint of desperation there. "And you're never even there anyway, between this place, your classes, and that library you practically live in."

"Who is it?" A truly horrifying thought worms its way into my brain. "Please tell me it's not that dude from your softball team who tried to mansplain to me why White Claw is basically the same as a hazy IPA."

Kasen takes another swig of scotch, looking anywhere but at me. "It's Banks."

The name hits me like a shot of cheap tequila—it burns going down and leaves you regretting everything. For a split second, I think I might actually stop breathing. "Banks Priestly?" My voice cracks, sounding way more panicked than I intend. "The guy with the ego the size of Mount Hood? *That* Banks?"

"The one and only." Kasen attempts this weak, hopeful smile that wilts under my death glare.

"Absolutely the hell not." I grab a bar rag and start scrubbing at the sticky counter. My brother's best friend has always been like a goddamn splinter under my fingernail. Living with him? That's a special kind of torture I *will not* be signing up for. "No freaking way. Never in a million years. Why can't he just crash at your place?"

"My place is still a disaster zone with the renovations, remember? I'm stuck in that tiny Airbnb by the river for the next couple of months. It's barely big enough for me, let alone another person."

"He's a goddamn firefighter! He makes decent money. He can afford a freaking hotel."

My brother actually scoffs, rolling his eyes. "You have no idea what firefighters actually make, do you?" He finishes off his scotch and slides the empty glass back across the bar, like he expects a refill. Fuck him. "His entire apartment building got flooded thanks to some idiot upstairs and a burst pipe. There's black mold everywhere. His insurance is being a royal pain in the ass, and he's been sleeping at the firehouse when he's not pulling double shifts covering for some poor bastard who broke his leg. He needs an actual bed and a shower that doesn't come with biohazards."

My traitorous brain immediately flashes back to the last time I laid eyes on Banks Priestly. Kasen's stupid birthday party three months ago. Me, four vodka sodas deep and feeling just a little too brave, letting my guard down for approximately two seconds to stare like an idiot while Banks laughed with his unfairly hot firefighter buddies. The way his plain white t-shirt stretched across shoulders that looked like they could carry a goddamn building.

The memory of that exact moment—how his eyes had locked onto mine across the crowded backyard, his annoyingly perfect lips curving into that smug, knowing smirk—still sends this unwelcome heat pooling low in my belly.

Three months later, and I can still hear his voice, all low and husky, when he caught me staring. The way he'd leaned in close enough that I could feel his breath tickle my ear as he whispered, "Take a picture, Freckles. It'll last longer."

The nickname had grated on my last nerve, almost as much as the involuntary goosebumps that had popped up all over my skin when his fingers had "accidentally" brushed mine as he took my drink from me and downed it as I watched. *Accidentally my ass.*

Heat crawls up my neck, making my face flush. I'd rolled my eyes and spun away, but the damage was done. He knew I'd been looking. And later, when I'd mentioned the business class I was struggling with...

"Still playing bartender until you find a real job?"

The casual dismissal of everything I've busted my ass to build at Ember, the assumption that my job is just some temporary pit stop—it had made me want to punch him in the face and then kick him in the balls just for funsies.

"No," I tell Kasen firmly, my voice leaving no room for argument. "Find someone else. Anywhere else." I lean forward, narrowing my eyes at him.

He's pulling out the big guns with the puppy-dog eyes, but I'm immovable. I will *not* be swayed. "He's got nowhere else to go, Clover. The fire station isn't exactly set up for someone to live there. They don't have enough beds, and the guy's running on fumes."

"Sounds like a 'him' problem, not a 'me' problem." I turn my back to him and start wiping down the back bar, needing to physically escape those guilt-tripping eyes of his.

"He'd do it for you."

A snort of laughter bursts out of my throat. "Banks Priestly wouldn't let me crash on his couch if I were homeless and bleeding in a blizzard with a pack of hungry wolves circling."

"That's total bullshit and you know it." Kasen's voice softens, and I hate everything about this. "He's always looked out for you."

"No, he's always looked *down* on me." I practically throw the wet rag into the sink, the splash echoing in the suddenly quiet bar. "There's a major difference."

"It's just until his apartment's livable again, I swear." Kasen pulls out his ultimate weapon—that earnest, pleading expression that somehow convinced our parents to let him keep that mangy, three-legged stray cat we found when we were kids. Even I'm not immune. "Three months, tops. Please, Clover. I wouldn't ask if there was any other option."

I cross my arms over my chest, racking my brain for any halfway decent excuse that won't make me sound like a total bitch. "My apartment only has one tiny bedroom."

"He can crash on the couch. It's surprisingly comfortable for a futon."

"I work crazy late. He works even crazier shifts. We'll be tripping over each other constantly."

"So, make some rules. You're practically the queen of rules." He's got me there. "Consider it a massive favor to me. I'll owe you big time—like, do your laundry for a month big time."

I let out a long, slow breath, my resistance finally crumbling under the weight of Kasen's relentless pleading and, if I'm being honest, my own stupid bleeding heart. Despite everything that annoys the crap out of me about Banks Priestly and his smug face, the thought of anyone—even him—having no place to go makes my stomach clench.

It doesn't hurt that he's stupid hot.

"Why can't he stay at the station? They have beds."

"They also have liability policies that say he can't be there when he's off duty."

"Fine," I snap, giving in with all the grace of a toddler denied a cookie. "But I have conditions."

The knot in my stomach tightens to the point I don't think it'll ever come undone, and my heart starts slamming against my ribs like it's trying to escape. Banks Priestly. Taking up all my space. The mere thought makes my skin prickle with this infuriating, unwelcome heat that I absolutely refuse to acknowledge.

Kasen's face splits into a relieved grin. "Lay 'em on me."

"Three months, and not a day longer. He stays the hell out of my way. Absolutely zero noise when I'm trying to study. He cleans up every single one of his messes. And absolutely, positively, no bringing random women back to my apartment." The mental image of hearing Banks doing the horizontal tango through my paper-thin walls makes my stomach churn like I just chugged a gallon of spoiled milk.

Nope. Nope nope nope.

"Done and done." Kasen rounds the bar and swoops me up in a hug, lifting me off my aching feet despite my undignified squawking. "You are officially the best sister on the planet. I'll text him and tell him it's a done deal. He can move in tomorrow."

"Tomorrow?!" I wiggle out of his suffocating grip. "I need at least a week to mentally prepare for this kind of torture—"

"He's been living out of a damn duffel bag for two weeks, Clover." Guilt, that sneaky little bastard, lands a direct hit courtesy of my brother. "His shift ends at noon tomorrow. I'll text you when he's on his way."

Before I can even think of a decent argument, he throws a couple of crumpled bills on the counter (barely enough to cover the Macallan, the cheapskate), and kisses the top of my head before practically sprinting toward the door, clearly terrified I'll change my mind.

"Kasen!" I call after him, my voice echoing in the empty bar.

He pauses with his hand on the door handle. "You seriously owe me so freaking big for this."

His grin is this perfect mix of gratitude and pure mischief. "I know. And hey, Clover? Try not to stab him in his sleep, okay? It's hard to make new friends and I like this one."

I flip him off and then he's gone, leaving me standing alone in the suddenly too-quiet bar, wondering what fresh brand of hell I've just willingly signed up for.

2
Clover

IT'S 2:18 AM, and I'm elbow-deep in a bowl of bread dough, kneading it with the kind of aggression usually brought on by the comment section on political posts.

But this here? This is Banks-induced agitation. You know what? Throw a little my brother's way, too.

Baking is my therapy. It's cheaper than therapy-therapy, and way more satisfying than just screaming into a pillow. The whole methodical process of measuring, mixing, and pounding usually manages to quiet the circus of crazy thoughts in my brain. Usually.

Tonight, not even the familiar rhythm of mixing and kneading the dough can shut up the full-blown rage-panic in my head at the thought of Banks freaking Priestly and his enormous firefighter boots stomping all over my life.

My apartment isn't exactly a palace—it's a slightly cramped one-bedroom in an old warehouse conversion with exposed brick that's constantly shedding and pipes that sound like they're having a very enthusiastic orgy when the heat kicks on——but it's *mine*. Every single inch of it screams "Clover," from my organized-by-color bookshelves to my perfectly arranged bar cart to my collection of plants, all named after classic cocktails. Mint Julep, my favorite, has prime window real estate where the morning sun hits just right.

Banks is going to disrupt all of this just by breathing. He's loud, probably leaves a trail of dirty socks wherever he goes, is definitely arrogant, and is entirely too large for normal human-sized spaces. His personality alone probably takes up more square footage than my entire damn apartment.

The dough beneath my knuckles bears the brunt of my Banks-and-Kasen-induced fury as I punch it down with enough force to make a professional MMA fighter wince.

"Stupid hot alphahole firefighter," I grumble to Moscow Mule, my awesome low-maintenance snake plant. "Stupid brother and his stupid guilt trips."

I could have said no. *Should* have said no. But Kasen knows exactly which emotional buttons to push to make me cave like a cheap tent in a hurricane.

He's always looked out for you.

The words echo in my head as I roughly shape the dough into a messy boule and practically shove it into a proofing basket. Has Banks really looked out for me? My mind grudgingly coughs up that one night in college at a frat party when this overly persistent dick wouldn't take "no" for an answer. How Banks, the chivalrous jerk, just appeared out of nowhere, his hand heavy on the guy's shoulder, his voice dropping to that low, dangerous rumble that always made the hairs on my arms stand up despite my better judgment. "She said no. Might want to listen before I *make* you listen." I'd been so pissed at his knight-in-shining-armor routine back then, insisting I could handle my own damn self.

I'd also been a little... yeah, no, we are definitely not going there.

Okay, so *maybe* he has looked out for me in his own special brand of irritating, alphahole way. But that doesn't give him the right to invade my personal bubble, use my tiny bathroom, see me in my ancient, holey pajamas, or witness my pre-coffee zombie state.

I carefully slide the banneton into the fridge for its overnight proofing and then get started on the cinnamon rolls. My famous, stress-induced, middle-of-the-night cinnamon rolls that Kasen would probably sell his own kidney for. The ones Navy pretends to hate me for bringing to work ("They go straight to my thighs, Clover!"), but still manages to inhale three before her shift even starts. Even Theo, who acts like he survives on nothing but green smoothies and smugness, suddenly develops an urgent need to chat with me whenever I bring them in.

By the time I finish the dough and set it to rise in a warm spot, it's closer to four than three. My hands smell like yeast and butter and cinnamon, and there's a light dusting of flour all over my black work pants, but I do feel a little better. I scrub my hands clean and survey my small but immaculate kitchen, wondering what it'll be like once Banks steps foot in here.

Will he leave dirty dishes in the sink? Empty coffee mugs glued to the counter? Wet towels forming a swamp on the bathroom floor? Will he silently judge my need for order the same way he not-so-silently judges my career choices?

"This isn't that bad," I tell myself, trudging toward my bedroom. "You can survive anything for three months, right?"

I try to convince myself of the lie as I yank off my work clothes and throw on an oversized t-shirt that's probably older than some of the guys who hit on me tonight at the bar.

I lie to myself as I aggressively brush my teeth.

Then I keep lying to myself as I set my usual number of alarms—one on my phone, one on the digital clock on my nightstand, and a third on my dresser across the room, strategically placed so I have to haul my tired ass out of bed to turn it off.

I'm still trying to convince myself as I finally slide between the cool sheets, my body aching from another Friday night in the trenches.

But even as sleep starts to pull me under, those unwelcome thoughts elbow their way to the front of the line: Banks freaking Priestly is going to see me first thing in the morning, hair looking like a bird's nest, eyes all puffy and gross, with morning breath wearing my favorite unflattering sleep shirt. My teenage crush, Banks Priestly, will be sprawled out on my futon when I stumble in after late shifts, probably shirtless because guys like him seem to be allergic to shirts. Banks freaking Priestly will be in my tiny apartment, breathing my air, using my shower, touching my stuff.

I groan and yank a pillow over my face, muffling a frustrated yell.

Three months. Ninety damn days. Two thousand, one hundred and sixty freaking hours.

Ugh.

3
Banks

I'M A GODDAMN MESS.

My best friend's had some stupid fucking ideas over the years, but this has gotta be his worst.

Living with his little sister for the next three months?

If he knew how bad I want to fuck her, I doubt he'd have been so quick to offer her couch up to me.

But turning down this opportunity would've been moronic, so here I am, lifting my shaking hand to knock on Clover James's door.

I've just spent forty-eight hours battling a four-alarm warehouse fire. My muscles are screaming, and my brain feels like sludge. Now I'm about to be face-to-face with the one woman in Portland who makes my heart pound like I've sprinted up ten flights of stairs in full turnout gear whenever she looks at me.

Kasen warned me she wasn't exactly thrilled about this arrangement. I was exactly zero percent surprised when he warned me to, and I quote, "Be on your best fucking behavior or she'll stab you in your sleep." Which is fair. The number of times I've deliberately gotten under Clover's skin just to watch her cheeks flush and her blue eyes narrow into that cute glare? I'd deserve it.

It's just so damn fun.

I adjust the duffel bag on my shoulder and knock three times, hard enough to be heard but not enough to seem demanding. The door swings open halfway through the third knock, and every coherent thought in my head just fucking vanishes. Gone.

She stands in front of me in a pair of criminally small sleep shorts and a tank top with a popsicle on it. Underneath, it says *It's Not Gonna Lick Itself* and fuck, my mouth waters. I'd give my right arm to lick it for her. Don't even care what part of her *it* is.

Her black hair is piled on top of her head in a messy bun that's listing dangerously to one side, a few strands escaping to curl against her neck. Without her usual makeup, the freckles across her nose and cheeks are fully visible.

The sight of her in those tiny shorts sends a jolt of raw, primitive hunger through me. My fingers fucking ache to grab her hips, to mark that pale skin with my mouth, my teeth, my hands. I want to claim her in ways that'd get me buried alive if Kasen ever found out. But goddamn it, I want her so bad it scares me.

She looks soft. Approachable. Nothing like the sharp-tongued bartender who rolls her eyes at my jokes and acts like I don't exist.

My throat goes dry. "Hey, Freckles."

Her eyes narrow. "Don't call me that."

I clear my throat, biting back the urge to rile her up. "Sorry." I'm not sorry, but I'm too fucking exhausted to deal with her wrath right now. "Clover."

She steps back, gesturing for me to enter with a stiff wave of her hand. My gaze snags on how her shirt rides up, exposing a sliver of pale skin and those indecent shorts that make my lungs seize. Feels like I just sucked in a lungful of smoke—every nerve in my body locks on that tease of bare flesh. I swallow hard before I embarrass myself.

I force my eyes up, catching the slight widening of her eyes as she takes in my appearance.

"You look like hell," she says and then bites her lip like she didn't mean to blurt out the first thought that popped into her head. There's something beneath the bluntness, too. Concern, maybe. Though she'd probably rather set herself on fire than admit it.

"There was a warehouse fire in the industrial district. Just came off a double." I drop my duffel inside the door and roll my shoulders, wincing at the protest from my overworked muscles. "Place went up like it was made of matchsticks and soaked in gasoline. We almost lost two guys when a support beam collapsed."

For a split second, the mask slips, and genuine worry flickers across her face. "Is everyone okay?"

"Yeah. We got 'em out." I leave out that I was one of the ones who went back in. That I can still feel the heat of the flames licking at my turnout gear, hear the roar of the fire as it consumed everything in its path. Or that I'd spend another forty-eight hours in that inferno if it meant someone's dad made it home to his kids.

She nods once, then produces a sheet of paper from nowhere. "These are the house rules. I expect you to follow them."

I blink at the color-coded bullet points. Jesus. She typed them out like a goddamn operations manual.

"You color-coded them," I say, a half-smile tugging at my mouth despite my exhaustion.

"Red for hard non-negotiables, yellow for important but flexible, green for preferences." She crosses her arms over her chest, which does interesting things to her t-shirt. Things I shouldn't be noticing if I want to keep all my limbs. "It's efficient."

I skim the list, my amusement growing with each item.

Rule #1: NO bringing women back to the apartment. EVER.

(Bold, underlined, and in red)

Rule #2: Quiet hours are from 8 AM-12 PM and 6 PM-9 PM.

(So she can sleep after her night shifts and studying, I'm guessing)

Rule #3: Wipe down all kitchen surfaces immediately after use.

(Not even a five-minute grace period?)

Rule #4: Do NOT move the plants under any circumstances.

Rule #5: If you eat any of the emergency chocolate stash, replace it within 24 hours or suffer dire consequences.

(Which, coming from a five-foot-four force of nature, could mean anything.)

"What counts as a 'dire consequence'?" I glance up from the paper to find her watching me closely.

"You don't want to find out." She tucks a stray strand of hair behind her ear. "Any questions before I show you where you'll be sleeping?"

I hold up the paper. "Do I need to sign this in blood, or...?"

"Don't tempt me, Priestly." But there's the faintest quirk at the corner of her mouth that might, if I squint real hard, be the ghost of a smile.

She leads me through the apartment, which is exactly what I'd expect from Clover James—spotless, organized, and much warmer than she pretends to be. There are exposed brick walls, bright throw pillows, and plants fucking everywhere. Every bookshelf is organized by color, creating a rainbow effect that somehow looks pretty instead of lame. The kitchen gleams with neat countertops and labeled canisters.

I'm almost afraid to touch anything.

"Bathroom's there." She points to a door off the living room. "My room is on the other side. The couch is a futon and pulls out into a bed. I set fresh sheets on the chair for you."

"Thanks." It's a simple gesture, but after two weeks of grabbing sleep on my buddy's dingy floor, I could kiss her for it. An actual bed sounds like heaven.

As much as I love to fuck with her, she really is doing me a solid here.

She shifts her weight from one foot to the other, and I notice she's barefoot. Her toenails are panted a sparkly blue. It's so unexpectedly intimate, seeing her guard down like this, that I have to look away before I pop a boner picturing all the things we could do naked.

Since apparently, I'm desperate enough for her that bare feet equal nakedness.

"Hungry?" she asks abruptly.

I realize I can't remember the last time I ate something. "Starving."

"I made sourdough last night. Grilled cheese okay?"

"You bake?" For some reason, this surprises me. How did my obsession with all things Clover not uncover that she likes to bake?

"When I'm stressed." Her eyes flick to mine, daring me to say something. If I wasn't so tired, I would. "I spent most of last night baking after Kasen dropped this 'Hey, my bestie's living with you now' bomb on me yesterday."

"I can find somewhere else—"

"It's fine." She waves me off like it's nothing. "I said yes, didn't I? It's done."

She moves into the kitchen, and I follow, watching this girl I've known since she was a mouthy teenager. I've seen Clover James roll her eyes at drunk idiots, slam down shots like water, and handle troublemakers with the same gives no fucks attitude she handles everything else with. But here in her own kitchen, there's a softness I'm not used to seeing as she pulls out bread, butter, and cheese.

She made homemade fucking sourdough, for Christ's sake.

"You can sit," she says, nodding toward the small table tucked against the wall. "Unless you want to shower first. You smell like a campfire."

"Hazards of the job." I run a hand through my hair, grimacing at the gritty feel. "I'll clean up after. If I jump in hot water now, I'm pretty sure I'll pass out face-first in my sandwich." I do get up and wash my hands, though.

She nods, her movements precise as she slices bread that looks like something from a magazine. "How bad was it? The fire."

Part of me wants to play it off, but there's an undercurrent of real concern in her voice that tugs an honest answer out of me.

"Bad. It was an old building with a shit ton of chemicals stored improperly. We're lucky it didn't spread to the neighboring structures." My eyes follow her hands as she butters the bread. Which, of course, makes me think of how her fingers would feel against my skin—something I definitely shouldn't be thinking about right now. "One of our probies got lost in the smoke. I had to go after him."

Her head snaps up, eyes wide. "You went back in?"

"It's part of the job," I say, shrugging like it's no big deal.

For a second, she just stares, something flickering in her gaze I can't pin down. Finally, she turns back to the stove. "That's... brave."

It's the closest thing to a compliment I've ever gotten from her. "Nah. Just what needed to be done."

Silence falls between us as she cooks, but it's not uncomfortable. I lean my head back against the wall, closing my eyes. The faint sound of bread sizzling in butter makes my stomach rumble. Even through the smell of smoke seeping off my skin—that stench that never quite leaves even after multiple showers—I catch the mouthwatering scent of toasting sourdough and melting cheese.

"Don't fall asleep at my table." Her voice jerks me back to consciousness. When I open my eyes, she's setting a plate in front of me. A perfectly golden grilled cheese cut diagonally. Steam curls up from the center where melted cheese threatens to spill out.

"This looks phenomenal." I bite in and damn near moan at the taste—crisp edges, fluffy center, tangy cheese. "Holy shit, Freckles. This is the best thing I've ever put in my mouth."

She sits across from me with her own plate, but she's not eating, just watching me. "It's just grilled cheese."

"Nothing about this is 'just' anything." I take another bite, savoring it. "Seriously, this bread? You made it from scratch?"

A faint pink tinges her cheeks. "Bread-making isn't rocket science. Time does most of the work."

"It's still impressive." I catch her gaze over the table. "You're impressive."

Her blush intensifies, but she slaps a brick wall over it fast. "Don't."

"Don't what? Compliment your baking?"

"Don't..." She waves a hand between us. "This. We're not friends, Banks. You're crashing here for three months, then you're gone."

I nod, swallowing another bite. "I'm aware. Doesn't mean I can't appreciate you and what you're doing for me."

She makes a dismissive noise and finally starts in on her own sandwich. I watch her eat—small bites, brow creased like she's working through something. She's wound so tight I'm surprised she doesn't snap in half.

"So," I say, filling the silence, "what's up with all the plants?"

Her eyes light up for a split second before she schools her face back to neutral. "They make me happy." She shrugs. "And for fun, they're all named after cocktails."

"Of course they are." I grin. "Which one's your favorite?"

"Mint Julep. Julie for short." She nods toward a plant on the windowsill. "He's a mint plant and he's been with me three years. He's survived a move and a spider mite infestation."

I have no idea what spider mites are, but they sound disgusting. "Nice." I want to keep her talking but I'm floundering for something to ask.

She fiddles with her glass of water. "I like them because they're simple. As long as you pay attention to what they need, they thrive."

"And what does Mint Julep need?" I'm pretty sure I've never given a damn about plants before. But Clover could be talking about paint drying and I'd still want to listen.

"Morning sun, plenty of water, room to spread his roots. And someone to talk to. Studies show plants respond to voices."

"You talk to them?" I can't hide my smirk.

She immediately bristles. "It helps them grow."

"I believe you," I say, raising my hands in mock surrender. "It's cute."

She stiffens. "I'm not cute."

"No?" I arch an eyebrow. "What's the preferred adjective? Badass? Intimidating? So obsessively organized it borders on clinically insane?"

She narrows her eyes. "You've been here forty-five minutes and you're already violating rule number six."

I squint at the sheet next to me on the table. "Pretty sure there is no rule six."

"That's 'Don't be an asshole.' It's implied."

I bark out a laugh, unable to help myself. Even half-dead on my feet, messing with Clover James is the best time I've had in weeks. "You're something else, you know that?"

"And you're deliberately trying to piss me off."

"Maybe." I polish off the last bite of my sandwich and lean back. "Or maybe I just like seeing that flush on your skin. And your eyes turn this shade of blue when you're mad. They're the exact color as the middle of a flame burning extra hot."

She blinks, mouth parting in what might be shock. "Are you… are you flirting?"

"Would it break one of those precious rules if I was?"

"Yes." She leaps to her feet, grabbing my empty plate. Her shoulders are stiff, but I catch the faintest tremor of something—nerves? "That's rule number seven. No flirting."

"Oh, so that one's official." I grin. "Not just implied?"

"Yes, it's going on the official list." She spins toward the sink, and part of me wishes she'd take that frustration out on me instead of the dishes. "Specifically for cocky firefighters who think they're charming when they're actually just obnoxious.

Now please go shower, you stink. Towels are under the sink. Don't hog all the hot water."

Rising from my chair, I realize just how cramped this kitchen is. If I stepped forward, I could box her in against the counter. Press closer, see if that sharp tongue of hers tastes like I've imagined.

"Thanks for the food, Clover." I force myself to give her space, even though I'd rather push her to see what she does. "And for letting me crash here. I know Kasen left you with no choice."

She doesn't turn around, but her posture relaxes the tiniest fraction. "You're welcome. Just follow the rules and we'll be fine."

Right. Follow the rules. If there's one thing I love, it's pushing boundaries. She doesn't need to know that yet, though. I'll let her find out the fun way.

I shut the bathroom door behind me with a soft click, duffel in hand. The place is immaculate, just like the rest of Clover's apartment, but it's got that unmistakably girly vibe—pale blue shower curtain, rows of little bottles without labels lining the counter, and a clean, fresh scent that's way too nice for a guy covered in two days' worth of smoke and sweat.

There's even a plant living on the windowsill.

It's a hell of a contrast to the station's locker room, that's for sure.

Catching my reflection in the mirror, I almost groan. No wonder she said I looked like hell. My eyes are bloodshot, streaks of soot cling stubbornly to my skin, and my hair's doing that stand-up-in-all-directions thing. The shadows under my eyes are so big they could get their own zip code.

I yank off my T-shirt and crank on the shower, waiting for the water to heat. My body aches in that twisted, satisfying way only a brutal fire can leave you with—like I got run over by a truck but somehow survived. It could've been so much worse today.

As steam fills the small bathroom, I strip the rest of the way and step under the spray. The hot water hits my shoulders, and I can't hold back a groan. Feels like heaven on sore muscles. I reach for one of her bottles—something that smells like citrus and vanilla—and try hard not to think about how this same soap glides over Clover's skin.

And fail. Miserably.

My brain conjures up this crystal-clear image of her in here, the water streaming over those full tits, that gorgeous black hair clinging to her neck, freckles everywhere, lips parted and head tipped back as she rinses soap from every inch of her body. Her hands sliding lower, exploring places I'd give anything to touch—

Fuck.

I twist the knob to cold so fast I curse, hissing as ice-cold water pelts my overheated skin. This is exactly the shit I can't be thinking about. Not when I'm bunking in her apartment. Not when I've spent years swearing to Kasen I won't look at his baby sister that way.

"Liar," I mutter, letting the frigid water nuke my libido.

Because the truth is, I've wanted Clover James since I saw her at seventeen, rolling her eyes at Kasen across some crowded house party like she owned the damn place. She was whip-smart, sharp-tongued, and so beautiful it physically hurt to lay eyes on her.

But I made a promise to my best friend. And Banks Priestly doesn't break promises—not to the people who matter.

Which is why the next three months are gonna be the sweetest kind of hell. Living under the same roof, sleeping in a room just one wall over from hers, watching her stroll around in tiny shorts, hair loose, guard down. Eating the food she cooks, catching whiffs of the scent that now clings to my skin everywhere I go.

I lean my forehead against the cool tile and let the water wash away the last of the grime, even if it does nothing for the heat still pulsing through me. Cold shower or not, I know one thing for sure:

I'm so completely, utterly fucked.

4
Clover

IT'S amazing how fast "short term" can turn into "feels like goddamn forever."

One week. Just seven measly days. That's all it's been since Banks freaking Priestly and his perfect face and firefighter muscles invaded my existence, and already my beloved routine has been tossed into a dumpster and set on fire.

Exhibit A: It's 5:41 AM—an ungodly hour where only bakers and serial killers are awake––and I'm standing frozen in my kitchen doorway, staring like a dumbass at a half-naked man making coffee in *my* kitchen when I should be blissfully unconscious.

"Morning, Freckles," Banks says without even turning around, like he's got some creepy sixth sense that alerts him to my presence. His back is to me, all broad shoulders and sculpted muscle that tapers down to a narrow waist. I can't see them right now, but there are abs. *Abs.* In real life. There's even one of those V things that are pretty much crack to every woman with a pulse.

And my pulse this morning just so happens to be between my thighs.

Oh, and as if this man wasn't hot enough, the early morning sunlight streaming through the window catches on a scar that runs along his left shoulder blade. The imperfection of it breaking up the miles of inked skin and muscles just makes him better somehow.

My brain immediately starts firing off a million questions about that scar. Questions that will remain forever unanswered, thank you very much.

"Don't call me that," I mutter, the response mostly involuntary by now. I force my sleep-fogged eyes away from the mouthwatering expanse of tattooed skin and focus on the absolute betrayal happening on my countertop. "Is that... Are you reorganizing my spice rack right now?"

Ugh. I can already feel that familiar twitch starting up in my left eye. This is going to be a long three months.

He glances over his chiseled shoulder, his lips quirking up at one corner in that charming half-smile that he totally knows is hot. "The way you had it was a mess. This way, everything you need for, say, Mexican night is all together. Makes way more sense."

"You touched my spices?" My voice goes up about three octaves with each word. "That's a direct violation of rule number eight!"

"Don't touch Clover's organizational systems unless you want to die," he recites, turning to face me with two steaming mugs of coffee that look almost small in his large hands. Hands I have never once fantasized about having on my body. "But I kinda took that more as a suggestion than an actual hard-and-fast rule."

I narrow my eyes at him, trying very, very hard to maintain eye contact with his greenish brown eyes that are more brown than green this morning, and not let my gaze drift southward to his chest. Or his abs. Or that damn V line that points directly to the promised land in his low-slung sweatpants. Or, you know, the very obvious outline of what's residing in those sweatpants. "I don't seem to recall adding an asterisk to that rule that said 'unless Banks thinks he knows better'."

He holds out a mug and it's my favorite one. It's got a gold rim and *sorry for what I said before I had my coffee* written in big, bold letters. Is that supposed to be some commentary on my pre-caffeine crankiness? *Asshole.* "Peace offering?"

My traitorous hands reach for the mug before my brain can even register what's happening. Our fingers brush during the exchange, and this wave of tingles shoots straight up my arm.

Seriously? Tingles? I've been doing the Olympics of social distancing all week just to avoid this kind of accidental contact, but Banks seems determined to invade my personal space every chance he gets.

"Thanks," I manage, taking a big gulp of the coffee to hide the flush on my face and can only hope he doesn't notice what my nipples are doing right now. I close my eyes and moan because this coffee is perfect—strong, with just the right amount of cream and a hint of cinnamon. Exactly how I like it. My eyes snap open and focus on Banks as he shifts behind the counter. "How the hell did you know how I take my coffee?"

He just shrugs, the movement causing his muscles to ripple under his skin. I could watch it all day. Just sit here sipping an endless supply of perfectly made coffee and enjoy the show. Wait, no. *Bad, Clover.* "I pay attention, Freckles."

Now what the hell does *that* mean? Something warm sparkles to life inside of me at his words. I immediately stomp on it. "Well, stop. And you better put every single spice back exactly where it was. Now."

"You'll thank me when you're trying to make some complicated curry next week and don't have to dig through a million bottles to find your garam masala."

"I hate Indian food."

He just grins, completely unrepentant, and takes a deliberate step closer, invading my already compromised personal space. "We'll see about that, Freckles. You've never tasted mine."

Was that flirty? It's not just me, right? It totally was.

I take another sip of my delicious coffee, trying to ignore the way my body is reacting to his mere presence. We're not even going to talk about what he just said. "Don't you own a shirt? Maybe I should add another rule to the list."

His grin widens, and his eyes do this slow, entirely too hot sweep down my body, lingering for a beat or two on my sleep shorts and tank top. I cross my arms to try to hide my nipples. "Nah, you won't do that. Know how I know?"

I shake my head.

"Your nipples are practically waving hello."

"They are so not—" *Okay, they definitely are.* Crap. I really hoped he wouldn't notice. I clamp my mouth shut, my cheeks burning. He's absolutely right, but I'd rather swallow a bottle of hot sauce than admit it. "It's cold in here," I snap.

His grin just turns even cockier while I glower at him. Is it possible to glower up at someone taller than you? I'm giving it my best shot. "Sure it is."

"Shut up. Go cover up... all of that." I gesture vaguely at his torso, which is basically a walking, talking anatomy lesson in muscle with ink drawing little maps to all the best parts.

"All of what?" He takes another step closer, crowding me against the counter like he's been doing all damn week. When we pass each other in the hallway. Reaching right past me for the remote so his arm brushes mine. Leaning over me to grab a glass from the highest cabinet when there were perfectly good glasses drying on the counter.

"You're not cute, Priestly."

"And yet you can't stop staring."

"I have to go shower." I sidestep him, clutching my coffee mug like it'll protect me from doing something incredibly stupid. Like reaching out and touching him.

Or jumping his bones. Bone. Whatever.

He smirks. "Because it's so cold in here?"

"Stop looking at my nipples, you perv!"

He completely ignores me. "I fixed your leaky faucet in the bathroom, by the way," he calls after me as I try to make my escape. "The washer was shot. And your showerhead was practically fossilized with mineral buildup. I soaked it in vinegar overnight, so you should actually have decent water pressure now."

I freeze mid-escape, turning slowly to face him. "You... fixed my shower?"

"Yep." He takes a casual sip of his coffee, like he didn't just blow my mind. No one's ever done something like this for me before. Not even my damn landlord and it's his job. "I noticed it was dripping, and the pressure sucked."

"I've been trying to get my cheap-ass landlord to fix that damn drip for months."

He just shrugs again, completely unfazed by what he's done. "It was a quick fix."

"Oh." I'm suddenly at a loss for words, which is a rare and unsettling occurrence. I'm not entirely sure what to do with this information or the weird, unfamiliar feeling that's starting to bloom in my chest. Is this... gratitude? Confusion? Wait, is this... *affection?*

Ew, no. Gross.

Setting *that* aside, there's also the disturbing realization that maybe having Banks around isn't going to be the complete and utter disaster I was anticipating. "Thanks," I manage, the word feeling a little awkward coming out of my mouth. "I guess."

"You're welcome, I guess," he mimics, that damn smirk back

on his mouth again, but his eyes are... warm. And something about the way he's looking at me makes it a little hard to remember how to exhale.

I haul ass to the bathroom before I do something truly idiotic, like smile at him or, God forbid, start thinking of him differently. I can't afford to do that, not when it took me years to get over my crush on him the first time. He is *not* allowed to worm his way back in like that by being nice to me. Nope. I just need a second to remind myself he's the cocky a-hole firefighter who thinks my life choices are less than impressive.

The bathroom door clicks shut behind me with a satisfyingly solid sound, and I lean against it, letting out a slow, shaky breath.

See? I'm fine.

Any lukewarm feelings that might've been developing are already gone.

I set my coffee on the counter and reach to turn on the shower, completely unprepared when a strong, steady stream of water immediately bursts forth. Huh. He actually did fix it. Maybe this three months won't be a complete and utter nightmare after all. Maybe.

Steam starts to fill the bathroom as I strip off my shirt and sleep shorts. I step under the spray and let out the biggest sigh of relief as hot water pounds down on me with so much more pressure than I've experienced in months.

As if summoned to disturb my moment of zen, a loud knock shakes the thin door.

"What?" I yell over the sound of the glorious water.

"Sorry!" Banks's deep voice comes through the door. "I forgot my razor in there. Mind if I grab it real quick?"

All that tension in my body that had just melted away comes right back. Before I can even form a coherent "Hell no, you can wait until I'm done," the door cracks open a few inches.

"I'm not looking, I swear. Just reaching in for it."

"Banks, don't you dare—"

Too late. His arm snakes through the gap, groping blindly on the counter. I press myself back against the shower wall, even though the curtain is completely opaque. The fact that he's literally right on the other side of that flimsy piece of fabric, that if he wanted to, he could just yank it back and see me naked and wet and...

My brain throws a goddamn circuit breaker at the mental image. Heat that has absolutely nothing to do with the water temperature floods through me, making my cheeks flush all over again.

"Got it," he announces, his arm withdrawing as quickly as it appeared. "Thanks, Freckles. Enjoy your shower."

The door clicks shut again, and I exhale the longest breath of my entire life. Enjoy my shower? What the hell was that tone he just used? And why am I suddenly analyzing the exact inflection of those three words? This is not good. Not good at all.

"This is fine," I mutter, reaching for my body wash. "Everything is fine."

Except nothing feels fine. I've spent the last seven days in this constant state of high alert. Hyper-aware of exactly where Banks is at all times. Hyper-aware of how he smells—like fresh air and smoke and expensive cologne. Hyper-aware of the sheer amount of space he takes up just by existing. And most disturbingly, hyper-aware of how my body decides to betray me whenever he's even remotely close.

Because I am *not* attracted to Banks Priestly. I refuse. That would be peak levels of self-destructive and goes against every single meticulously planned step of my life, which does not, in any way, shape, or form, include falling for arrogant, know-it-all firefighters.

Nope. Not happening. Absolutely not.

By the time I finally finish my shower, throw on some

clothes, and emerge from the bathroom, Banks has thankfully put on a shirt—a faded PFD one that stretches across his chest in a way that's almost worse than him being shirtless. It looks soft and I want to steal it as soon as he takes it off, but no.

No, Clover.

It looks like while I was having an existential crisis in the shower, he whipped up eggs and toast and is now sitting at my kitchen table, looking far too comfortable and at home in *my* space.

"I made breakfast," he states, like I'm blind and haven't noticed the perfectly cooked eggs and golden-brown toast sitting in front of me. And seriously, what the hell did he need to interrupt my shower for if he was just going to leave that sexy shadow of stubble on his jaw? I swear he did it to rattle me. Well, mission fucking accomplished, Banks. "You mentioned having an early class today."

I did mention that. Once. In passing. Like, three days ago. I hate that he remembers little details like that.

"Thanks," I say, sliding into the chair across from him. "But you really don't have to cook for me."

"I know I don't *have* to." He pushes the plate closer with a smirk on his face, almost like he knows he's getting to me. "I want to. Consider it part of the rent."

"You're already paying actual rent." Like, real, honest-to-goodness money that he insisted on giving me, even though Kasen told him it wasn't necessary.

"Yeah, well." He shrugs, and the movement does these utterly unfair things to his shoulders under that shirt that, yep, I'm totally stealing later. "I eat a lot. Might as well cook for you, too, while I'm at it."

We fall into this almost... comfortable silence as we eat. It's unnerving how quickly we've fallen into these little routines. Him making coffee in the mornings after his early shifts. Me baking at night after my late ones. Him getting way too invested in the trashy reality shows I watch to de-stress. Me pretending not to notice when he leaves his books on fire-fighting history scattered on my coffee table, always bookmarked with random scraps of paper covered in his surprisingly neat handwriting. It's all... weirdly domestic. And I don't like it one bit.

I don't like how much I like it.

"I might be working late tonight," I say, breaking the silence between us that's more comfortable than I thought it'd be. "It's inventory day at Ember."

He nods, reaching for his coffee mug. "I'll be at the station until six, then I'm meeting Kasen for a beer. I can swing by Ember after if you want to walk home."

"I don't need a chaperone, Banks."

"Did I say you did?" His eyes flick up to meet mine, and they're suddenly intense and impossible to decipher. "Maybe I just want to see if Navy's invented any new cocktails I should try."

I know he's lying. He's a beer man like my brother and Navy's drinks are usually over the top with dirty names like *the squirter* and *rim job*. He's worried about me walking home alone in the dark, the same way he's been "coincidentally" showing up right around closing time all week. But arguing with him is exhausting, and I'm already running late for my class.

Plus, I got about three hours of sleep so I don't have it in me to fight.

"Whatever," I mutter, pushing back my chair and grabbing my bag. "Just don't flirt with Navy. She'll eat you alive, and I'll have to listen to her brag about it for weeks."

I'm going to pretend that's the only reason I don't want him flirting with Navy and it has absolutely nothing to do with the weird, uncomfortable little twist I feel in my gut at the thought of Banks and Navy... you know. Touching. Or kissing. Or fucking.

That little twist has now morphed into full-blown murder fantasies about both of them.

Something is *seriously* wrong with me.

His low chuckle follows me as I head for the door, almost like the arrogant jerk can read my mind. "Wouldn't dream of it, Freckles. See you later."

5
Clover

"YOU'RE ACTING ALL TWITCHY TONIGHT," Navy observes as she lines up shot glasses. Her eyes, though, are locked on me. "And you've checked your phone like a million times in the last hour."

"I'm not twitchy," I protest, shoving my phone back into the pocket of my apron. I've just been checking the time... a lot.

"Uh-huh. And I don't reread my favorite graphic novels until the pages fall out," she deadpans, tipping the bottle of tequila upside down across the shot glasses. "Spill."

"There's nothing to spill. I'm just counting down the minutes until we close, okay? Inventory days are always brutal and I'm about to crash."

Navy's eyes narrow into these suspicious little slits. "Nah, it's something else. You're always tired. It's your natural state." She spins to set up a tab for a young guy who checks out her ass and I roll my eyes. "You've been acting weird and distracted all week." She suddenly gasps, pointing a dramatic finger in my direction. "You're getting some, aren't you? That's totally what this is!"

"What? No, I am absolutely not!" The bottle of Aperol I'm

holding nearly takes a nosedive onto the sticky bar top. "Why in the hell would you even think that?"

"Because you've got that 'I'm getting the good dick and can't wait to have it again' look. Who is he? I'm dying to know who got you to break your personal best dry spell record."

"I am *not* hooking up with anyone," I hiss, glancing around nervously to make sure none of the other bartenders or the owner, Theo, are within earshot. "And it hasn't been that long, so shut up."

"Thirteen months and counting." She waves her phone at me before sticking it in her back pocket. "I put an entry in my calendar."

"You did what?"

Navy winks, grabbing a bottle of gin. "I knew you'd argue with me at some point. Now I've got the receipts."

I let out a dramatic sigh, knowing there's no way Navy's going to let this go. She's like a bloodhound with a scent when it comes to gossip. It's even worse when it involves me and my non-existent love life. "Fine. If I tell you, you have to swear you won't make a huge deal out of it."

"Huge deal? Me? Never. Now, continue. And leave nothing out."

I take a deep breath, bracing myself for the big deal she's about to make. "Banks is... staying at my apartment for a little while."

Navy fast blinks about twenty-five times as she processes this information. She lets out this dramatic gasp that makes a few of the people sitting at the bar glance over at us. "Banks Priestly?! As in, your brother's gorgeous firefighter friend who you've been not-so-secretly drooling over since you were practically a fetus?"

"I have not been drooling—" I cut myself off at her raised eyebrow that calls me on my bullshit. "Fine. Maybe there was some mild, totally age-appropriate attraction when I was a hormonal teenager that I have since completely outgrown. His apartment flooded, and Kasen guilt-tripped me into letting him crash on my futon for a couple of months."

"A couple of *months*?" Navy's shrieks. Thank god for loud music. Her face splits into this wide, delighted grin. "Oh, this is pure gold. The sexual tension between you two could probably power all of Portland."

"There is no sexual tension," I insist, even as my cheeks start to feel suspiciously warm. "There is only regular, run-of-the-mill tension because he's annoying and arrogant and he had the nerve to reorganize parts of my kitchen."

"He *what*?" Navy bursts out laughing, grabbing a bar towel to wipe imaginary tears from her eyes. "Oh, honey, he's totally that kid on the playground pulling your pigtails because he's got a crush. That's adorable."

"It is not. He's driving me insane." I grab a cloth and start wiping down the already gleaming bar top with unnecessary force. "And he walks around shirtless. And fixes things without even asking. And he somehow manages to make coffee exactly how I like it." I realize I'm only making her point for her and snap my mouth shut.

"Sounds horrible," Navy says, not even trying to hide the massive smirk on her face. "How will you go on with a hot, tattooed handyman who makes you perfect coffee and wanders around half-naked? My deepest condolences on your truly awful situation."

"You are so not helping right now."

"I'm not trying to help," she says, bumping her hip against mine with a knowing smirk. "I'm trying to get you to admit you've got it bad for Firefighter Priestly."

"Well, I don't," I lie through my teeth, feeling my cheeks heat up anyway. "I have to tolerate him for three months, and he's gone. Then I can get back to my life."

"Uh-huh. Keep telling yourself that, sweetie. Just make sure you give me all the juicy, embarrassing details when you inevitably end up 'accidentally'," she makes air quotes, "slipping and 'accidentally' falling on his dick."

Thankfully, our first wave of Friday night customers chooses that exact moment to descend upon Ember, and soon the bar is slammed, preventing any further interrogation from my best friend. Friday nights are always a chaotic blur of spilled drinks, loud music, and even louder conversations, and tonight is no exception. I lose myself in the familiar rhythm of shaking cocktails, chatting with the regulars, and trying to keep everything from descending into utter madness.

It's nearly midnight when the hair stands up on the back of my neck and I know he's walked in.

Since when can I feel his presence before I ever see him?

Banks slides onto a stool at the far end of the bar, looking good enough to attract the attention of almost every woman in the bar in his dark henley that stretches across his broad shoulders like it was personally tailored to showcase his biceps. His jeans are doing things to his thighs that Instagram models only dream of. His hair is still damp from a shower and they're messy in that *I just fucked someone* way he has. He catches my eye across the crowded bar and offers this small, almost shy wave, and yup. There goes my heart—and that pulse between my thighs.

He doesn't try to flag me down for service. Instead, he starts chatting with my boss, Theo, who actually looks like he's enjoying a conversation for once. That's almost as surprising as Banks fixing my shower.

I try my best to ignore his presence, but my awareness of him is like this constant, annoying tug, my eyes magnetic as they keep getting drawn back to him whenever I'm not actively dealing with a paying customer.

Once, I catch him watching me mix some complicated, multi-step cocktail, his gaze tracking the movement of my hands with an intensity that makes my skin prickle in a way that has absolutely nothing to do with annoyance. Heat crawls up my neck, and I have to resist the urge to fidget.

"What can I get for you?" I ask when I finally manage to make my way down to his end of the bar, aiming for professional detachment and probably landing somewhere closer to flustered mess.

"Just a beer. Whatever you've got of Timber's on tap." His eyes don't leave my face for a second, and I get this distinct, unsettling feeling that he's seeing way more than I want him to. "Good crowd tonight."

"It's Friday," I say with a casual shrug that feels anything but casual, pulling the tap for Kasen's go-to IPA. "How was your shift?"

"Quiet, thankfully. Just a couple of medical calls and some idiot who thought pulling the fire alarm for fun was a good idea." He accepts the beer with a nod of thanks. And then, of course, his fingers have to brush mine during the exchange, again, and I'm pretty sure he's doing it on purpose now. "Oh, and Kasen says hi, by the way. He's still stuck at Timber dealing with some kind of distribution fuck up."

I nod, already scanning the crowded bar for my next customer, when I notice some entitled douche at the other end getting increasingly aggressive with Navy. His body language is all kinds of wrong – leaning way too far over the bar, jabbing his finger in the air, his voice loud enough to carry over the music.

"Excuse me," I murmur to Banks, already moving toward the brewing storm.

"I said I want to talk to you!" the guy is slurring as I approach. He's huge, his face is blotchy red, and he's clearly had one too many. "Why won't you just give me your damn number?"

Navy's glaring at him and it takes a lot to get her to drop her customer service smile. "Like I've already told you, I'm not interested. Can I call you a ride?"

"I'm not going anywhere," he snaps, his eyes bugging out. "I want your number. And for you to stop being such a fuckin' tease."

"Is there a problem here?" I step in, positioning myself in front of Navy. I've dealt with my fair share of drunk, entitled assholes in my years slinging drinks and I've got thick skin.

The guy swivels his attention to me, his bloodshot eyes narrowing into these squinty little slits. "Who the hell are you?"

"I'm the manager," I say, keeping my voice even. "And I think it's time for you to wrap it up and head out."

"I'm not finished with my drink."

"Yeah, you are." I nod my head toward Marco, our security guy who's built like a brick shithouse and probably bench presses small cars for fun. "You can either walk out on your own two feet, or Marco here can help you. Your choice, buddy."

The dude leans forward, getting all up in my personal space, and his breath smells like stale beer, making my eyes water. "Listen, you little bitch—"

"She said you need to leave." Banks's voice has dropped about ten octaves and is now this low, dangerous rumble that vibrates with barely leashed aggression. His whole body has gone rigid, shoulders squared, jaw tight. It's like watching Dr. Jekyll turn into Mr. Hyde, only so much hotter. "I suggest you get the fuck out of here before I make you."

But the drunk idiot doesn't seem to realize he's about to pick a fight he can't win. Instead, he just snorts dismissively and reaches out his giant paw to grab my wrist. "I just wanna talk to the pretty bartender—"

His words cut off in a strangled gasp as Banks moves faster than I've ever seen anyone move. One second he's leaning against the bar, the next he's got the guy's wrist in a grip so tight I can practically hear the bones grinding.

"Touch her again, and the only thing you'll be walking away with is a stump," Banks says, his voice eerily calm despite the murderous glint in his eyes. He's not yelling, not making a scene, but the absolute certainty in his tone makes every single hair on my body stand on end. "That's not a goddamn threat. That's a promise."

The drunk guy's face goes completely white as Banks leans in close, his voice dropping so low I have to strain to hear his next words.

"She's not interested. She will never be interested. And the only reason you're still standing right now is because causing a scene in her bar would piss her off. Now get the fuck out before I decide her feelings on that matter less than teaching you some manners."

Banks releases the guy's wrist with a little shove, and the dude stumbles backward, clutching his arm and shooting Banks a look that's a mix of fear and pure, unadulterated rage.

"Whatever," he mutters under his breath. "This place is probably full of lesbians anyway."

He snatches his jacket off the back of his stool and storms out, nearly bowling over a group of women who are just walking in.

"You okay?" Banks asks, his intense gaze sweeping over my face like he's checking for damage. It makes my skin prickle in that weird way it does lately around him.

"Yeah, I'm fine," I say, irritation and this other, warmer feeling that I am absolutely not going to acknowledge right now bubbling up inside me. I turn to Navy, who's already back to wiping down the bar. "You good?"

She just nods, already moving to serve the next customer like nothing even happened. "Yeah. Thanks, you two."

Banks stays beside me for another tense moment, his large frame close enough that I can feel the heat radiating off him. "I didn't mean to overstep, Freckles."

"Then why the hell did you?" I snap, keeping my voice low so the remaining customers don't get an extra dose of drama with their last call. "I had it handled."

"I know you did." His eyes are locked on mine, that intense gaze making it hard to breathe. "But I couldn't just stand there and watch him talk to you like that. And when he touched you—"

"Go sit down, Banks. I'm working."

He holds my gaze for one more beat, then finally nods and heads back to his stool. I immediately throw myself into serving the remaining customers, deliberately avoiding his end of the bar for the rest of the night as I silently fume over his whole knight-in-shining-armor thing. My body definitely appreciated it, but my brain? My brain is currently staging a full-blown revolt. Does he honestly think I'm incapable of handling some drunk idiot? That I need him to swoop in and rescue me like some damsel in distress?

I scoff out loud, earning a questioning look from a customer as I ring him up.

By the time last call is announced and the last stragglers are finally heading out, the tight knot of anger in my chest has solidified into something sharper and more uncomfortable.

6
Clover

IT'S after 2 AM when we finally lock up. Navy, bless her observant heart, takes one look at my face and offers to handle closing. "Go home, Clover. You look like you're about two seconds away from committing a felony."

Banks is waiting outside, leaning against the brick wall of the building with his hands shoved deep in his pockets. The streetlight catches on his jawline, highlighting the stubble that's somehow gotten even sexier throughout the night because he clearly didn't bother to shave this morning after interrupting my shower to get his razor. Which, for some reason, just pisses me off even more.

He straightens up when he sees me.

"I figured you might want some company on the walk home," he says.

"What I want," I say, starting down the street at a brisk, angry pace, "is to not be treated like I'm some fragile little thing who can't handle a drunk idiot."

He falls into step beside me, his longer legs easily matching my furious stride. "I never said you couldn't handle it, Freckles."

"You didn't have to say it. Your actions said it loud and clear."

The cool night air does absolutely nothing to cool down my simmering frustration. "I've been dealing with obnoxious, drunk guys since I started bartending. I don't need you charging in like some goddamn white knight."

"It wasn't about you needing me, Clover." His voice is low and careful, like he's trying really hard not to piss me off more. "It was about me not being able to just stand there and watch some jackass disrespect you like that. Especially when he put his hands on you."

"But that's exactly the goddamn problem!" I whirl around to face him, the words exploding out of me. "You don't get to decide when I need protecting, Banks! Just because you're bigger and stronger doesn't give you the right to step in whenever the hell you feel like it!"

"That's not what this is about, Clover."

"Oh, really? Then enlighten me. What's it about?"

Banks stops walking, his expression shifting, hardening into this fierce, almost possessive look that makes the tiny hairs on my arms stand up. "It's about the fact that I've been looking out for you since you were seventeen years old. Don't expect me to suddenly stop now."

I stare at him, my mouth hanging slightly open, completely and utterly speechless for a second. "What in the actual hell are you talking about?"

He runs a frustrated hand through his already messy hair. "Why do you think those entitled frat guys suddenly left you alone your freshman year? Or why the bartender at O'Malley's who wouldn't take no for an answer suddenly found a job across town? Or why your handsy Econ professor took that unexpected 'sabbatical'?"

The pieces of the puzzle click into place with this sickeningly clear *thunk* in my brain.

"You've been... interfering in my life?" My voice rises with each word, going from disbelief to full-blown fury in about two seconds flat. "Behind my back?"

"I promised Kasen I'd look out for you, okay?" He takes a step closer, backing me right up against the brick wall of a café that's closed for the night. The rough brick scrapes against my back through my thin shirt. "After your mom died, he was worried about you. Said you'd gotten reckless, that you were taking all kinds of stupid risks."

"So what? You've been my secret bodyguard all these years?" Anger surges through me, hot and furious, and I've never wanted to punch someone in the face more in my entire life. "Do you have any freaking idea how unbelievably insulting that is?"

"It wasn't like that."

"Then what was it like? Please, enlighten me."

His hands come up, pressing against the brick wall on either side of my head, effectively trapping me. His body is so close I can feel the heat radiating off him, smell that familiar mix of fresh air and smoke that clings to his skin, mixed with his delicious cologne. His eyes drop to my mouth, and for one heart-stopping, terrifying moment, I think he's going to kiss me. My lips part involuntarily, my breathing going shallow and uneven as I desperately try to remember all the very good reasons why that would be a catastrophic idea.

"I promised your brother I'd protect you," he says, his voice dropping to this low, rough whisper that sends a shiver straight down my spine. "But don't for one goddamn second think that's the only reason I can't keep my eyes off you." His gaze flickers back up to mine, and there's a raw intensity in his eyes that makes my knees feel a little weak. "There's nothing brotherly about what goes through my head every single time you walk into a room, Clover James."

My breath catches in my throat. The anger that was just boiling inside me suddenly turns into something else—something hot and undeniable that's begging me to reach out and close the small distance between his body and mine. His admission hangs in the cool night air between us, and *ho-ly shit*.

I can feel his breath ghosting across my face, see the frantic pulse hammering in his throat. If either of us dared to move even an inch, our lips would be touching. The mere possibility sends a jolt of pure electricity through my entire body, making me hyper-aware of every single point where we're almost, but not quite, making contact.

Before I can decide what I'm going to do, he abruptly pushes himself away from the wall and starts walking again, leaving me standing there frozen in place while I try to get my shit together.

"You coming, Freckles?" he calls over his shoulder, his voice rough around the edges. Yeah, he was just as affected by that as I was. Am.

I follow him in stunned silence, my mind racing a mile a minute as I try to make sense of the bomb he just dropped. Did Banks Freaking Priestly just confess to having actual, non-brotherly thoughts about me? After years of teasing me and basically treating me like his little sister? After apparently playing some kind of secret guardian angel in the shadows of my life?

We reach my apartment building without exchanging another word. The silence between us is thick enough to cut with a knife, charged with everything that was just said and everything that was left hanging in the air. Every step feels like navigating a minefield of emotions I am so not equipped to handle. Banks unlocks the door and holds it open for me, his hand lingering on the doorknob. I brush past him, totally tuned it to every single molecule of air that separates our bodies.

"Clover," he says quietly as I make a beeline for my bedroom.

I pause in the doorway, not even bothering to turn around.

"I'm exhausted, Banks. Whatever this is, it can wait until tomorrow." And honestly, I don't think I'm strong enough to stop tonight if we get close to each other again. I need to rebuild my defenses.

Thankfully, for once, he doesn't push. "Good night, then."

I close my bedroom door behind me and lean against it, letting out a shaky breath. "Well, Mojito," I mutter to the sword fern plant thriving on my windowsill, "your girl is officially in deep, deep shit." I've been having one-sided conversations with my plants since college—partly because some study I vaguely remember said it helps them grow, but mostly because they're the only living things I know who don't talk back or judge my questionable life choices. "I can't keep doing this. He's everywhere. Touching everything. Looking at me like... like..." I trail off, realizing I'm gesturing wildly like some kind of lunatic.

Eventually I give up on working out my thoughts with my plant and crawl into bed. But does sleep come easy? Nope. Instead, I lie wide awake, staring blankly up at the ceiling, listening to the sounds of Banks moving around in the other room. The quiet clink of a glass in the sink. The soft, almost silent padding of his bare feet across the living room floor. The groan of the futon as he settles his huge body onto it.

And then, of course, my brain decides this is the perfect time to start wondering what it would be like to have him in here with me. In my bed. With his hands all over me, his big, solid body pressing me down into the mattress, crowding me until he's the only damn thing I can see. The only thing I can feel.

God, what the hell is wrong with me?

The wall separating my bedroom from the living room suddenly feels thinner than a sheet of paper. He's *right there*, just on the other side, probably lying awake too, staring up at the ceiling just like I am. Is he replaying what he said? About what could've happened if either of us decided to move even an inch?

Is he lying there regretting his confession, or is he plotting exactly what he's going to say when we talk about it tomorrow? And why in the ever-loving hell can't I stop hoping he *doesn't* regret it?

I roll onto my side, punching my pillow. This whole arrangement was supposed to be temporary. A simple, no-big-deal favor for Kasen that would last three months, and then my life would go right back to normal. Instead, one freaking week in, and everything is completely upside down. My routine, my personal space, years of diligently practiced 'I don't want to bang my brother's best friend *at all*' denial—all of it dismantled with just one stupid sentence.

And the scariest part of all this? The part that I can barely even admit to myself in the dark, silent safety of my bedroom?

I don't want him to stop looking at me the way he did tonight, like I'm some precious, maddening puzzle he suddenly wants to solve. Like he's wondering what I'd sound like if I were screaming his name. I don't want him to take back a single word about what goes through his head when he sees me. In fact, I kind of want to hear more. Every single explicit, underwear-soaking detail.

I'm up and halfway through my third batch of cinnamon rolls before I even realize what I'm doing. There was absolutely no way sleep was going to happen with the way my thoughts were spiraling out of control. Banks is passed out on the couch and I'm trying to be quiet, but he must've been tired enough that he's sleeping through everything.

Flour dusts my arms up to my elbows, and the kitchen counter has completely disappeared under a chaotic landscape of mixing bowls and measuring cups. Baking usually manages to calm my frazzled nerves, but tonight my hands won't stop shaking. Banks Priestly has not only invaded my apartment but has also set up permanent residence in my brain, and the only way my subconscious knows how to deal with it is to bake enough pastries to feed a small army.

"He'll be gone in less than three months," I whisper, needing to hear the reminder out loud so it really sinks in. "You can do this."

If I'm being honest with myself, there's a growing feeling that there's no timeline in which Banks *doesn't* leave some kind of permanent, irreversible mark on me. And I'm just really, really afraid I'll never be able to move on.

7
Banks

THREE THINGS in life are guaranteed: death, taxes, and Captain Bill Morgan chewing your ass out the second you so much as blink wrong.

"Priestly!" His bark slices through my mental fog like a chainsaw through butter. "What the hell was that? You trying to kill yourself and Foxton?"

I blink, disoriented, suddenly realizing I'm standing in the training yard with my harness half-buckled and zero clue how I got here. Brenna's dangling from the tower, perfectly secured for the rescue drill, giving me serious side-eye. The rest of the crew is dead silent.

"Sorry, Cap." I fumble with my equipment, snapping the buckles tight. "Got a little distracted."

"A little?" Morgan's thick eyebrows angle together over eyes that've seen too much tragedy to tolerate carelessness. "You're supposed to be anchoring Foxton, not daydreaming about whatever has you walking around with your head up your ass today."

Heat crawls up my neck. All I can think about is last night. The walk home with Clover, the way I cornered her against that wall, the words I spat out before my brain caught up to my mouth:

There's nothing brotherly about what goes through my mind when you walk into a room.

Jesus. Her face afterward—shock, confusion, maybe something else—has been stuck on an endless loop in my head ever since. Neither of us even said goodbye this morning. I left for my shift at five, and we both pretended we were too busy to talk about it.

"You want to tell me what's going on?" Morgan's tone drops low so the rest of the crew can't hear. "Or should I bench you now, before you get someone killed?"

I straighten up, forcing myself to focus. "I'm good, Cap. Won't happen again."

His gaze drills into me, not buying it for a second. "My office when we're done."

That's not a suggestion. I give a tight nod and force myself to run through the motions. We finish the drill without further screw-ups, but I can feel Morgan's stare burning holes in my back the whole time.

An hour later, I'm perched in front of him in his cramped office—walls plastered with decades' worth of crew photos and commendations. I've been in this hot seat before, usually for taking too many risks on calls. Never for being so lost in my own head I forgot how to do a damn anchor.

"Out with it," Morgan says, leaning back in his creaky chair. "What's got you so distracted you can't remember basic protocol?"

I consider bullshitting him—maybe a story about insomnia, or the fiasco with my apartment. But Morgan's bullshit detector is a finely honed weapon after twenty-plus years in the department.

"I'm staying with my best friend's sister while my place gets fixed," I admit. "It's... complicated."

A flicker of understanding flashes across his weathered face. "Ah. You sleeping with her?"

"What? No!" *Not yet.* I drag a hand over my face, flustered. "It's not like that."

His raised eyebrow practically calls me a liar to my face.

"Fine. It's exactly like that, except we're not actually sleeping together." I lean forward, elbows braced on my knees. "I've known her for years. She's always been off-limits. But now that we're living together..."

"It's testing your self-control," he finishes, "and you're so busy thinking about what's under her clothes, you're forgetting there's a team depending on you."

When he lays it out like that, it sounds downright reckless. Which, yeah, it is.

"Either get your head in the game or get your ass on the bench," Morgan says, voice firm but not unkind. "Distracted firefighters become dead firefighters, Banks. You know that better than most."

The image of my dad's turnout coat floods my brain—hanging in my old closet, the folded flag on Mom's mantle. The high price you pay when anything goes wrong in this job.

"I got it," I say, squaring my shoulders. "Won't happen again."

"Good." He nods. "Now go do an equipment check on Engine Three. Might help sweat out some of that pent-up energy you're carrying around."

I recognize a dismissal when I hear one. I stand, and he calls my name right as I'm at the door. I turn back.

"For what it's worth," he says, a rare glint in his eye, "some of the most dangerous fires are the ones worth running into."

It's about as close to relationship advice as I've ever heard from Bill Morgan. I give a tight nod and leave, determined to clear my head.

I don't make it ten feet before Brenna corners me at the lockers.

"I'm gonna need you to start talking. Now," she demands, arms crossed. That's such a Brenna thing to demand. No lead-in. Just straight to business.

There's something about Brenna Foxton that reminds me of Clover—she's got that same no-nonsense attitude, same fierce determination to prove herself in a place that doesn't always welcome her. Maybe that's why I end up telling her the truth.

"My apartment flooded," I say, busying myself with my gear. "Then got mold. I'm crashing at Kasen's sister's place until it's fixed."

Brenna's eyes spark in recognition. "Clover, right? She runs that swanky cocktail bar, right?" At my surprised expression, Brenna grins. "Portland's small, and the female firefighter network is thorough. We've had our girls' night there once or twice, at Ember. That woman makes a gin fizz that'll change your life."

"That's her," I confirm, focusing a little too hard on checking my harness.

"Holy shit." Brenna's grin widens as she leans against the lockers. "You've got it bad for her, don't you? That's why you were so distracted today. Morgan had to yell your name three times before you heard him."

I glare at the locker door. "I don't 'have it bad' for anyone."

Except the part where I want to hang a sign around her neck that says 'Property of Banks Priestly' and dare anyone to challenge it. But I don't tell Brenna that.

She snorts. "Please. You look like a guy who's had a taste of what he wants and can't stop craving the entire damn menu."

I slam the locker shut with more force than necessary. "We haven't—there's no 'tasting' happening."

She cocks her head, studying me. "Yet. But you want it to,

58

right? Does Kasen know you're mentally undressing his sister on the regular?"

I open my mouth to deny it, but her pointed stare kills the words. "...No. And let's keep it that way."

"Because?"

"Because Kasen would kill me. And because I promised him I'd look out for her, not try to get in her pants."

Brenna levels me with a long stare, her expression softening. "Looking out for someone and caring about them aren't mutually exclusive, you know."

"It's complicated."

"Only because you're making it that way." She punches my shoulder, just hard enough to sting. "Women like her don't want a babysitter—they want someone who chooses them. Over and over. Who thinks she's capable of taking care of herself."

Her words slam into me like a kidney shot. "That's... surprisingly insightful."

"I'm full of surprises." She winks. "Now do us both a favor and figure your shit out before our next drill. I don't feel like plummeting to my death just because you're too busy imagining your landlord naked to clip my harness right."

Before I can fire back, the station alarm blares—three short tones for a non-fire emergency. The dispatcher's voice kicks in: "Engine 12, Truck 12, respond to a possible gas leak, 412 Northwest 21st Avenue."

My stomach lurches. That's Ember's block.

All chatter dies as we lunge for our gear and move toward the apparatus bay. I'm on Engine 12, second seat behind Captain Morgan. We screech out of the station with lights and sirens, and I hammer at the mobile data terminal, looking for details.

"Gas odor reported at the bakery next to the cocktail bar," I relay. "Manager called it in twenty minutes ago."

Morgan nods, weaving through traffic. "Full evacuation protocol. Priestly, Foxton—evacuate the surrounding businesses. Vetter and I will coordinate with the gas company."

"Copy." I clamp down on the surge of panic. Gas leaks are no joke—odorless except for the rotten-egg additive, and all it takes is one stray spark to blow the block sky-high.

We roll up seven minutes later. The baker's staff are huddled on the sidewalk, but pedestrians are still strolling by the other stores like nothing's wrong. My gaze locks on Ember, and my pulse jacks through the roof. It's just after four, so Clover's probably inside, maybe clueless there's a time bomb next door.

I'm out of the rig before it fully stops. "I'll take the bar," I bark at Brenna, not giving her a chance to argue.

I catch the faint stench of mercaptan halfway to the entrance. That rotten-egg smell is enough to set my teeth on edge. The second I push through Ember's door, I spot Clover behind the bar. She looks up, eyes widening at the sight of me in full gear.

"Banks? What—?"

"There's a gas leak next door," I cut in, adrenaline spiking. "We're evacuating the whole building. Now."

She doesn't waste time arguing. "How bad?"

"Bad enough to clear everyone out. You need to get at least a block away."

Her chin lifts in that take-no-prisoners way I've come to love and hate. "Navy, get the back door locked up and meet us out front," she calls to her coworker. Then her voice carries to the handful of customers. "Ladies and gentlemen, we're going to need you to please gather your things and exit the building. Your drinks are on the house. There's a gas leak next door, and we need you out of the building ASAP."

She's got this no-nonsense authority that leaves zero room for debate and that voice does things to me. Dick getting hard things. Even in a crisis, she's cool as ice, and I can't help feeling a surge of pride watching her handle it.

"Any pilot lights? Stoves? Water heaters?" I ask, eyeing the back bar.

"In the kitchen," she says, already heading that way. I follow—no chance I'm letting her go alone.

In the kitchen, she quickly turns off the gas to the range while I check my monitor. The readings are elevated but not in the explosive range—yet.

"All clear in here," I tell her. "Let's move."

We head back out front, and the block has already turned into controlled chaos. My crew's roping off the sidewalk, and the gas company just arrived, bright safety vests on. Clover stands next to me as I guide her across the street, my hand pressed to her lower back. I'm on duty, but damned if I'm not touching her in this moment.

"How long do we need to stay out here?" she asks, scanning the scene. There's tension in her shoulders, the wheels in her head spinning a mile a minute.

"Could be hours," I admit. "They have to find the leak, fix it, and then we sweep every building before letting anyone back in."

She nods, already thumbing on her phone. "I need to call Theo. And check if Navy got everyone out safely."

I leave her there to get an update from Morgan, my mind torn between the job and the urge to keep her glued to my side. Ten minutes later, I circle back and find her corralling the neighboring business owners like she's run citywide evacuations her whole life.

"They're saying at least three hours," she explains, voice carrying above the chatter. "The gas company's searching for the source, and the fire department will test each building before they give the all-clear."

A chef in a stained coat looks panicked. "We've got perishables—"

"No one's going inside until it's safe," Clover answers firmly. "The captain said once it's contained, they'll allow one person per business to lock things down."

I hang back, letting her take charge. This is a Clover I've never quite seen—levelheaded, commanding, stepping up to keep everyone calm and informed. It's sexy as hell, honestly, and I feel my dick give a twitch at the worst possible time.

Yup. Even in the middle of a potential explosion, I'm gone for her. There's no escaping it now.

For the next couple hours, I bounce between handling my assigned duties and swinging by the evacuation zone to check on things. Every time I head back, Clover's at the center of the chaos—arranging coffee for displaced customers and staff, negotiating with neighboring businesses to share outdoor seating, even wrangling a local band into giving an impromptu show on the sidewalk. Anything to keep people calm and entertained while they wait.

"You're pretty damn good at this," I say the one time I catch her alone, leaning against a streetlight with a clipboard she must've snagged from somewhere.

She looks up, a flicker of a smile tugging at her lips. Her hair's up in one of those messy buns I've only ever seen in the mornings back at her place. "Crisis management's basically bartending on a Friday night with bigger stakes."

"Somehow I doubt most bartenders would handle a gas leak evacuation like you."

"Most bartenders haven't been running their own space since they were twenty-two." She shrugs, but there's no bravado in it. "How's it going on your end?"

"They found the leak—some faulty line to one of the appliances. The crew's fixing it now. We'll start clearing buildings in the next hour." I hesitate, then decide to lay it on her. "You've really impressed a lot of people today, including my captain. He wanted to know who 'the general in the black shirt' was."

A soft flush climbs her neck, and she ducks her head. There's a stray tendril of hair teasing her cheek, and I clench my fist so I won't reach out and tuck it behind her ear. "I'm just doing what needs to be done."

"That's what makes it impressive, Freckles."

She doesn't roll her eyes at the nickname this time—just fixes me with a look I can't interpret. There's something crackling in the space between us since last night, a tension that sparks like static whenever we're close. I'm about to push it further when my radio crackles.

"Priestly, we're starting building sweeps," Morgan's voice barks. "Take Ember and the bookstore next door."

"Copy that," I reply, my gut twisting as I step back. "Duty calls. I'll find you when your building's clear."

She nods, already turning to talk to a group of business owners who all look desperate for answers. I force myself to focus on the job.

8
Banks

IT'S another hour before I can finally give Ember the green light. By then, it's past seven, prime time for the evening rush. Clover's short-staffed—it's just Navy and another bartender, Chris, who just made it in.

"Josie called out," she explains, flipping on the lights behind the bar. "Something about bad sushi and food poisoning."

My shift technically ended an hour ago, but instead of heading home after I checked out at the station, I came back here. Now, I'm hovering in Ember's doorway, watching Clover orchestrate a chaotic reopening. "Need a hand?" The question leaves my mouth before I can talk myself out of it.

She pauses mid-grab for a gin bottle, one eyebrow lifting. "You know how to bartend, Priestly?"

"I can pour a beer without embarrassing myself. And I'm a fast learner."

She weighs me with her gaze, clearly deciding whether I'm more trouble than I'm worth. Finally, she nods. "We could use the help until the night crew gets here at nine. But you follow my lead."

"Yes, ma'am." I strip off my hooded sweatshirt, left in the black tee I had on underneath, then scrub my hands at the sink.

"You'll work service well," she instructs, pointing me to the side of the bar where drinks get made but not served directly to patrons. "Navy'll take orders; I'll handle the main bar. You cover the basic stuff—beer, wine, simple mixed drinks. Think you can handle that?"

"Pretty sure I can manage pouring liquid from one container into another without a catastrophe." I grin at the annoyed little twitch her mouth makes, and the way her eyes shine under the bar lights as she glares at me.

"We'll see." She tosses me a bar towel. "First rule: keep your station clean. Second rule: don't overthink it. Third: when in doubt, ask."

"Oh good, more rules."

She flips me off and I laugh, but she's the boss here. I may give her shit, but I'll behave.

So for the next hour, I do just that—pour beers, pop wine bottles, mix easy requests—while Clover does her thing like a pro. It's more intense than I expected: juggling multiple orders, staying in sync with Navy, making sure everything's labeled right. Watching Clover is mesmerizing. She somehow keeps three or four cocktails going at once, chatting up customers, and managing this well-oiled bar machine.

The bar's narrow, so we're constantly brushing past each other, reaching for bottles or glassware. Every accidental touch lights up my skin. At one point, she slips behind me to grab vermouth and her back presses against my chest—I stifle a groan at the jolt of need that rips through me.

"You're in my way, Priestly," she murmurs, but her tone's more sultry than irritated. The kind of heat that has nothing to do with annoyance. I move aside, but not before I catch the faint pink on her cheeks.

"Tight quarters back here."

"You being built like a damn linebacker doesn't help." She snags a shaker from the shelf, her arm brushing mine. "You're doing okay, by the way. For a rookie."

Coming from Clover, that's basically a standing ovation. "I have a good teacher."

Her gaze flashes up to mine. It's warm, almost surprised, and it makes my heart thud harder than it should. "There's a table asking for an Ember Old Fashioned. Want me to show you how to make our signature drink?"

"Absolutely."

She shifts closer, placing herself between me and the bar so I have to look over her shoulder to see. The pressure of her back against my chest spikes my temperature about ten degrees. I bite my cheek to keep from groaning when her ass brushes against my dick. "Start with the glass—an Old Fashioned tumbler." She sets it down. "Now a sugar cube."

I manage to drop the cube in, even though half my blood is currently rushing south. The tight space and the scent of her shampoo—fresh and citrusy—turns my brain to static.

"Three dashes of orange bitters," she says, grabbing the bottle. Instead of handing it over, she covers my hand with hers, guiding me as I shake bitters onto the sugar. Her fingers are soft and warm against mine. Having her between me and the bar, caged in by my body while she shows me how to make her signature drink—it's the sweetest kind of torture. Every cell in my body is screaming to turn her around, pin her against the counter, and claim that smart mouth. To make it clear to every man in this place that she's off limits.

But I don't. Instead, I stand there, every muscle tense, letting her lead me through the motions.

"Muddle it," she instructs, handing me the wooden muddler. Our fingers tangle a second before she pulls away.

"Not too hard. We just want the sugar dissolved, not to shatter the glass."

I nod, but my gaze is locked on the curve of her neck. All I can think about is how I want to kiss her there. Suck a mark into her skin. She must feel how hard I am—there's no way she doesn't. Any second now, I'm gonna lose it and do something that gets me stabbed or fired or both.

Fuck, she's going to kill me. Or her brother's going to when he finds out I'm into his little sister. I don't know how much longer I can hide it.

"Now muddle it," she instructs, pressing the wooden muddler into my palm. Our fingers tangle briefly before she withdraws. "Not too hard. You want to dissolve the sugar, not pulverize the glass."

For now, though, I follow her order, muddling the sugar and trying not to think about how good her lips would taste if I turned her around and kissed the fuck out of her. Because damn if she isn't worth all the trouble that'll follow.

"Now the whiskey," she says, her voice dipping lower. "Two ounces, exactly."

She hands me the jigger, and I pour the amber liquid with more care than I've ever shown anything in my life. Our fingers brush again, and this time there's no mistaking it—she's either fucking with me, or she wants this as bad as I do.

"Ice," she continues, leaning around me to grab one large, crystal-clear cube from the well. "We use a single large cube for less dilution."

When she slides that ice into the glass, her back stays pressed against my chest for a few too many heartbeats. The heat of her body radiates through her thin shirt, and I'm half convinced my heart's about to leap straight through my rib cage.

"Finally, the twist," she murmurs, a little breathless. She takes an orange peel and shows me how to press the oils over the drink, then rubs it along the rim before dropping it inside. "And that's our Ember Old Fashioned."

She turns in the circle of my arms, the drink behind her on the bar. We're close enough that I can count the freckles on her nose, see the darker flecks in her blue eyes. Her lips part, gaze dipping to my mouth.

For a heartbeat, I'm sure she's about to close the distance and kiss me. Her pupils are blown wide, cheeks flushed pink, breath coming quicker than normal. My entire body coils, ready to catch her mouth with mine. Her tongue flicks out, wetting her bottom lip, and it almost snaps my control. My hand clenches so hard on the bar's edge that the wood groans under my grip.

"Clover? A word, please."

We jolt apart like kids getting caught making out in the janitor's closet. Theo, Ember's owner and Clover's boss, stands at the end of the bar with a smirk as he eyes us. Clover clears her throat, and in the blink of an eye, she's all business again, smoothing her shirt and refusing to meet my eyes.

"Coming." She brushes past me, and I swear her hands are shaking, but I can't be sure. "Take that Old Fashioned to table seven," she calls over her shoulder. "Then you've got a gin and tonic, another G&T, and a vodka soda."

I track her with my gaze, watching the subtle sway in her hips, the elegant curve of her neck as she leans in to hear whatever Theo's saying. An ache lodges in my chest—an awareness that what I'm feeling isn't just about wanting to get her under me. I mean, that's definitely part of it, but it's also the way she took charge earlier, how people automatically looked to her for guidance. It's the gentle patience in her hands when she was teaching me this drink, and the flicker of vulnerability in her eyes when she almost—almost—gave in.

I'm falling for Clover James. No parachute, no backup plan, just free-falling. And if I do, I'm risking everything: Kasen's trust, my promise to watch out for his sister, not fall in love with her. Once I cross that line, there's no undoing it, and the scariest part is how little I care.

Navy sidles up next to me, snapping me out of my head. "You're screwed, Firefighter." Her grin is equal parts smug and sympathetic. "I've never seen her give anyone that look before."

"What look?" I can't help asking, even though I already know the answer.

"Like she can't decide if she wants to slap you or climb you like a goddamn tree." Navy snatches the ticket from my hand and starts mixing the drinks I'm supposed to be making. "If I had to bet? She's going for the tree."

I face the bar again, trying to force my brain onto the job instead of the words Navy just dropped. But my attention keeps drifting toward Clover, who's deep in conversation with Theo, her brow creased in concentration.

She glances up, and for a split second, the mask falls. Hot, raw hunger flickers in her eyes, and then she shuts it down, looking away.

Yeah, I'm in so much trouble here. And I'm not sure I give a damn.

9
Clover

THIS IS BAD.

This is so, *so* bad.

I'm starting to forget what my life looked like before Banks.

Two weeks into this whole sharing-my-space-with-my-brother's-best-friend-and-also-my-teenage-and-maybe-now-crush situation, and I've somehow stopped counting down the days until he leaves. Stopped drawing those invisible, but very important to my sanity, boundaries around my personal space. Stopped even pretending that I'm not hyper-aware of his every move, every breath, every damn time he clears his throat.

Which is, again, so bad.

"You're overthinking it again, Freckles," Banks says from across my tiny dining table, his deep voice cutting through the chaotic mess of my thoughts. "The concept really isn't as complicated as this textbook is trying to make it."

I glare daggers at my Business Analytics textbook, silently wishing it would spontaneously combust into a pile of useless, knowledge-repelling ash. "Easy for you to say. You're not the one with a final project due in, oh, let me check... three freaking days."

"True." He takes a long sip of his coffee—his third cup tonight, which should make sleep impossible for a normal human being, but the man could probably doze off in the middle of an earthquake. "But this is basically just applied statistics with a bunch of unnecessarily fancy words thrown in. I took it for my engineering major."

I look up at him, my brain momentarily short-circuiting as I try to process this new, completely unexpected piece of information. "Wait. You have an engineering degree? Since when?"

He just shrugs those unfairly broad shoulders, the movement causing his worn, soft-looking vintage Tool t-shirt to stretch across his chest in a way that sends an inconvenient little pang straight to my ovaries and dries out my mouth. "Since about seven years ago. When I went to college," he eyes me like I'm dense, "with your brother."

"But... you're a firefighter." *Duh, Clover, way to state the obvious.*

"Wow, Freckles, you *are* observant." His lips quirk up in his half-smile that does this unholy things to my body.

"I graduated, worked for a corporate firm downtown for about eight miserable months, hated every single second of being stuck behind a desk staring at spreadsheets, and decided to follow in my dad's footsteps instead."

I just stare at him, genuinely surprised. In all the years I've known Banks, he's always just been Kasen's cocky, perpetually unserious firefighter friend with the easy smile and that permanent five o'clock shadow. The guy who teases me mercilessly and looks way too good in his uniform.

Not... this.

Not a man who can casually explain complex data visualization concepts while making it sound like he's talking about the weather. Not someone who willingly gave up a cushy office job to run headfirst into burning buildings because it felt more meaningful.

"Why didn't I know that about you?" The question just slips out.

His eyes meet mine across the small table, and there's this unexpected flicker of something soft, almost vulnerable, in them. "You never asked."

The simple, honest truth of his answer lands in my stomach like a lead weight. He's right. In all these years, I've never really asked Banks anything real about himself. I've been so busy keeping my guard up, maintaining my armor against his relentless teasing and that impossible attraction that I've never been able to fully escape that I never bothered to look any deeper.

I guess I was too afraid of what I might find.

"Okay," I say, pushing my textbook aside and leaning forward. "Well, I'm asking now."

His eyebrows shoot up in genuine surprise. "Alright then, Clover James. What exactly do you want to know?"

"Everything." The word tumbles out of my mouth before I can overthink it and clam up. "Start with why engineering. Then why you decided to ditch that for running into burning buildings. Then just... work your way forward from there."

A slow, genuine smile spreads across his face, transforming his features from just being unfairly handsome to something genuinely devastating. "That might take a while."

I glance down at my phone. It's 10:28 PM. My final project isn't due until Friday, and right now, in this moment, actually getting to know the person sitting across from me feels a hell of a lot more important than working on my regression analysis.

"Lucky for both of us," I say, leaning back in my chair, "I've got time."

And so, over the next hour, Banks starts telling me his story. How he was always good with numbers and had this weird knack for spatial reasoning even as a little kid. How his dad, who only had a high school education, had really pushed him to go to college and pursue engineering, wanting him to have more opportunities. How college was a constant financial tightrope walk, but he somehow managed with scholarships and working a million part-time jobs. How that first and only corporate gig left him feeling hollow and empty inside despite the decent paycheck.

"The day I finally quit, my dad was so confused," Banks says, a laugh bubbling up at the memory. "He'd drilled into my head that I needed that degree, that it was my ticket to a better life. When I told him I was applying to the fire academy, he honestly thought I'd lost my damn mind."

"So what changed his mind?"

Banks's expression softens again, becoming almost sweet. "He saw me after my first week of training. Said he'd never seen me look that alive before." He runs a hand through his hair. "He died proud of me, at least. That's something."

My heart clenches at his words. I've known about his dad's death—Kasen had gone to the funeral, and I remember how quiet and shaken my brother had been when he got back—but Banks and I have never actually talked about it. "I remember when it happened. Kasen was really torn up about it for you. I just... we never really talked about it."

Without thinking, I reach across the table and cover his hand with mine. His skin is warm and calloused in places, and holy crap, what am I even doing right now? My heart does this little leap the second my skin makes contact with his, but it would look bad if I just yanked my hand back, so I take a deep breath and just... lean into how right it feels to touch him.

"No, we didn't," he murmurs, his thumb brushing over my knuckles, sending unexpected little bursts of electricity all the way up my arm. "It wasn't exactly the kind of conversation we usually had."

"I'm sorry, Banks," I say, and I actually mean it, more than I would have expected. "That must've been awful. Losing him like that."

He turns his hand over, our palms pressing together, and then his fingers slowly intertwine with mine. It's the first time we've touched on purpose, without the flimsy excuse of reaching for the same remote or awkwardly brushing past each other in the kitchen.

And just that single point of contact sends an intense heat spiraling through me, through every vein and blood vessel, all the way down to focus between my legs. It's like he's somehow managed to touch every single inch of me all at once.

"It was." His fingers tighten around mine, and a big part of me wishes he would just keep holding on forever. "But it's part of the job. We all know the risks when we sign up."

The casual way he says it—like his life being in constant danger is just some accepted fact of life—makes a horrible ache start in my chest. I think back to that gas leak at Ember, the way he didn't hesitate before charging in. How many other times has he run straight toward danger while everyone else was running the other way?

"What about you?" he asks, his voice softer now, breaking into my thoughts. "You never really talk about your mom."

I stiffen. It's a knee-jerk reaction to pull back, but his grip on my hand tightens just enough to let me know he's not letting go that easily.

"You don't have to," he adds, his eyes searching mine. "I'm just... I want to know you, Clover. The real you, not as my best friend's off-limits little sister who makes me think all kinds of things I shouldn't."

A surprised laugh escapes me despite the sudden heavy turn in the conversation. Yeah, I'm just going to pretend I didn't hear that last part, even as my internal temperature just went up by at least ten degrees. "She used to make these ridiculously elaborate cocktails for her book club. They were totally amateur with way too much sugar and the weirdest garnishes you've ever seen. They were disgusting." My lips curl into a reluctant, fond smile at the memory. "I'd sneak sips when she wasn't looking, which is probably why I ended up working behind a bar in the first place."

Banks's smile is gentle, and I can't seem to hold his gaze with the way he's looking at me. I shift in my chair, crossing and then uncrossing my legs.

I take a deep breath. "She got sick my sophomore year of high school. You already know this because of Kasen, but it was cancer. She went from diagnosis to gone in about five months." The familiar ache rises in my chest. It's duller now after eleven years but never completely absent. "Kasen took it really hard. I'm sure you remember."

"Yeah. He ended up dropping out that whole semester to help with everything."

I nod, remembering the blur of those months.

"And you?" Banks prompts softly, his thumb now rubbing slow, soothing circles around the inside of my wrist, and yeah, I think I might be melting right here at this table.

"I became super mom." The bitter little laugh that comes out of my mouth doesn't sound like me. "It was suddenly all up to me to keep the house running. I made sure Kasen ate something other than ramen. Got straight A's because that's what she would have wanted." I swallow past the sudden lump in my throat. "Control just kind of became my coping mechanism, I guess. If I could just keep everything in perfect order, then maybe nothing else bad would ever happen."

Banks's hand squeezes mine. "Is that why you hate it when I move your stuff or leave a mess?"

The question startles a laugh out of me. "Yes, you monster. That's exactly why."

"Noted," he says softly, his smile warm, his eyes never leaving my face. My toes curl into the worn rug under the table at the way he's looking at me. "And for what it's worth, I think your mom would be incredibly proud of you. Running the hottest bar in Portland, working your ass off on your business degree, handling everything the way you do? That's impressive as hell, Freckles."

His words hit me hard, threatening to go straight to my head and make me do something stupid. I can't help it; the question just claws its way out of my throat. "Is that what you really think? Because at Kasen's birthday party last year, you said I was 'just playing bartender until I found a real job.'" The words were so upsetting at the time, they did a great job of getting rid of my crush on him.

He winces, running a hand through his hair again and tugging on the ends. "Christ, did I actually say that? All I remember is being buzzed and trying not to stare at you all night." His eyes lock on mine, serious and completely unguarded. "I've always thought you were incredible at what you do. Anyone who's seen you run that bar knows it's not just some job to you. It's your damn domain. Your passion."

"Then why say it?" I press, needing to hear the reason.

"Because I'm a goddamn idiot who says stupid shit when I'm nervous around an insanely gorgeous woman I can't have." He shrugs, a hint of his teasing grin returning, but it doesn't quite reach his eyes. "It's always been easier to try to push you away than to admit how incredible you are."

No one has ever put it quite like that before. Usually, people focus on how I need to "chill out" or "take a breath" or whatever other patronizing bullshit they think will magically fix me. Banks is the first person who's ever looked at my drive as something to admire instead of something to correct, and I didn't even realize how much I needed to hear that until this very second.

"Thank you," I whisper, my voice coming out breathless. I clear my throat, desperately trying to regain some semblance of composure.

A massive clap of thunder crashes outside, startling both of us. I hadn't even noticed the storm rolling in, too caught up in our conversation. As soon as the thunder fades, rain starts to beat against the windows in a sudden, violent downpour. Wind kicks up and howls through the narrow alley beside my building, and the old windows rattle in their frames.

"Well, that came out of nowhere," Banks says, finally letting go of my hand to walk over to the window. The spot where his hand was feels cold, and I have to restrain myself from reaching for him again like some kind of desperate addict. "The weather app said it'd be clear all night."

"Yeah, well, predicting Portland weather is always a shitshow," I point out, joining him at the window. A flash of lightning illuminates his profile—the strong line of his jaw, the slight, almost imperceptible bump in his nose from where Kasen accidentally broke it during a backyard hockey game when I was sixteen. I remember bringing Banks ice packs while trying my hardest to pretend I wasn't staring at him. He's standing so close to me right now I can feel the heat radiating off his body, reminding me of all those years I spent trying my best to not notice how much he affected me.

"We should check the—"

The apartment plunges into darkness mid-sentence as the power cuts out.

10
Clover

"SHIT," I mutter, blinking as my eyes try to adjust to the sudden blackness. "Storm or the apocalypse?"

A blinding flash of lightning followed immediately by a deafening crack of thunder that rattles the windows answers that question.

"Definitely leaning toward apocalypse." Banks chuckles, his voice suddenly much closer than I expected. "You have any candles stashed away somewhere?"

"Kitchen drawer, the one right next to the sink. And there should be a flashlight in the hall closet."

I can hear him moving through my dark apartment with surprising confidence, especially considering he's only been crashing here for two weeks. My eyes slowly start to adjust to the minimal light filtering in with the occasional flashes of lightning through the windows. It's just enough to make out vague shapes but not any real details.

"Found 'em," Banks calls out from the direction of the kitchen. The distinct scratch of a match breaks the silence and the darkness, followed by the warm, flickering glow of candlelight. He reappears in the living room with several lit candles balanced precariously on small plates, setting them down on various surfaces around the room.

The flickering light casts dramatic shadows across his face, emphasizing the sharp angles of his cheekbones and the fullness of his lower lip. He looks like every single bad decision I've ever wanted to make, all wrapped up in romantic firelight. I am officially in so much trouble.

"You okay, Freckles?" he asks, catching me staring.

"Yeah, fine. Just..." I scramble for literally anything to say that won't end with me throwing myself at him. "I'm not exactly a huge fan of thunderstorms."

He watches me for a long moment in the flickering light before finally nodding slowly. "I'll grab that flashlight then."

By the time he comes back, I've already scurried around and collected every single candle I own from my bedroom and bathroom, desperately needing to keep my hands busy with something other than reaching for him. The storm continues to pound against the building, which pretty much mirrors the chaotic riot currently happening in my head. My phone chimes with a notification, saving me from having to come up with any more awkward conversation.

"The power company says it could be awhile," I report, glancing down at the notification on my phone. "Apparently, a transformer blew a few blocks over after it got a direct hit from lightning."

"Good thing you're so prepared." Banks tosses the flashlight onto the coffee table with a soft thud and then sinks back onto the couch, patting the empty spot right next to him. "Come here, Freckles. You're shivering."

Am I? I glance down at my arms, and sure enough, there's a fine layer of goosebumps all over my skin. But it's definitely not from the cold.

I hesitate for all of maybe two seconds before another loud boom of thunder makes the decision for me. I drop down onto the couch next to him, trying my best to maintain at least a sliver of distance between us. Fat chance when he takes up half of the couch—our thighs bump, sending a shock through me that has absolutely nothing to do with the raging storm outside.

"We're getting pretty good at this," Banks says, his voice dropping low enough that it vibrates through where our bodies are pressed together.

"At what? Surviving power outages?"

"Talking. Being real with each other for once." The flickering candlelight turns his eyes into this liquid gold color, and I have to force myself to look away before I do something incredibly stupid. "Two weeks ago, you were scaling the walls to avoid being alone in the same room with me. Now look at us."

He's right. Everything has shifted since that night outside Ember when he backed me against that wall and confessed all those dirty thoughts he's been having about me. Since I watched him walk confidently through that gas leak evacuation. Since I felt him standing behind me at the bar, his chest pressed against my back while I showed him how to make an Old Fashioned.

"Don't get used to it," I say, trying for flippant but landing somewhere closer to turned on. "This is just temporary insanity. Blame the storm and the fact that I'm currently trapped here with you."

He lets out a low laugh. "Sure thing, Freckles. Whatever helps you sleep at night."

We fall quiet, listening to the relentless assault of rain against my windows. His thigh is radiating heat against mine, and without meaning to, I find myself leaning just a little closer to him. The worst part is how right it feels, how my body instantly relaxes against his solid frame like it's been waiting for some kind of permission to finally let go.

"So, when did the whole color-coded bookshelf thing start?"

he asks out of nowhere, his voice a low rumble that's almost drowned out by the storm.

I blink at him. "What?"

"Your books." He gestures with his head toward my rainbow-arranged shelves. "You've got them organized by color. I was just curious when that whole system began."

I could totally lie, make some lame joke about Pinterest or aesthetic Instagram feeds, but the darkness and the steady, comforting warmth of his body right next to mine somehow make the truth just... slip out easier. "After my mom died. Her books were just everywhere, no organization whatsoever." I swallow hard, the familiar ache in my throat making an unwelcome reappearance. "I spent pretty much the entire week of the funeral just sorting them while Kasen dealt with all the actual important stuff. It just... gave me something I could control, you know?"

Banks just nods, not offering some canned sympathy line or a bunch of probing questions, which I appreciate more than he probably knows. "What about the plants then? You know, your little green babies." He smirks at me, and I have to shift because I can feel that dirty grin all the way down to my damn toes. "With their cocktail-themed names. White Russian is my favorite, by the way."

I laugh because of course he'd love the struggling Monstera. It needs the most care and I've learned that Banks has a total hero complex. "It started in college." A sudden crack of lightning illuminates the entire room for a split second, making me jump. Banks's hand lands on my shoulder, and I try not to focus on how big and warm it feels through my t-shirt. "My dorm room felt like some kind of sterile hospital—with white walls, white furniture, absolutely zero personality. I got this sad little ivy plant my first week and just named it Manhattan after the first drink I ever successfully made. Having something alive in there made it feel a little less like I was sleeping in a morgue."

Thunder booms outside, rattling the windows again as the rain continues to pelt against the glass.

"It makes sense that you'd name them after cocktails," he says, his fingers now absently tracing slow circles on the back of my neck. But every tiny movement, every point of contact, sends little jolts of electricity dancing across my skin. "It's very... you."

"What about you, Priestly?" I shift slightly to face him, which is probably a mistake because now we're close enough that I can make out the tiny flecks of gold in his eyes. "Got any weird organizational quirks I should know about before you start rearranging more of my stuff?"

His laugh rumbles low over the sound of the storm. "Nothing too neurotic, I promise. Though I do have a pretty specific system for my turnout gear back at the station." He's still tracing those damn circles on my neck, and I wonder if he even realizes he's doing it. "Everything has its exact place so I can get dressed in under thirty seconds when the alarm goes off. It's life or death, you know?"

I try to picture Banks at his locker back at the station, meticulously placing each piece of his gear, knowing that someday those precious seconds he saves might be the only difference between walking out alive and not coming home at all.

"Does it scare you?" I ask. "Running into fires? Especially after what happened with your dad?"

His jaw tightens, the muscle there flexing in the flickering candlelight. "Not the fire itself, not really. It's the unknowns that get you. A floor that gives way without any warning. A backdraft you can't predict." His fingers move from the back of my neck to my hair, gently twisting a strand around his finger. "The fear is a good thing, though. It keeps you sharp. The guys who start thinking they're invincible are usually the ones who don't make it home."

Just then, another bolt of lightning cracks right outside my window, followed immediately by a deafening clap of thunder that shakes the entire building. I startle against him, and his arm slides around my shoulders, like it belongs there, pulling me into the solid, comforting warmth of his side.

"Hey, thunder can't hurt you," he whispers, his lips so close to my ear I can feel his breath disturbing the tiny hairs there, sending a shiver cascading down my spine.

I really should move away. Put some much-needed space between us. That's what the sensible, rational version of me would do. But his body is so solid and warm pressed against mine, he smells so damn good, and somehow it just feels right to be tucked against him while the storm rages on outside.

"Tell me something," I say. "Distract me."

"I sleep better when I'm here," he says, and the way he blurts it out makes me think he didn't mean to admit it. I wonder if he'll stop, but he doesn't. "It's enough knowing you're in the next room. The nightmares don't happen as often."

I look up at him, finding his eyes in the dim light. "What nightmares?"

His chest expands with a deep breath, then slowly falls as he exhales. "There was a building collapse a couple of years ago. I was pinned under a support beam for almost three hours before they finally dug me out." His voice is surprisingly matter-of-fact, but his arm tightens around me, his fingers pressing a little harder into my skin. "I still wake up sometimes feeling like I'm trapped."

"I had no idea." And I really should have. How the hell did I not know something like that happened to him? Apparently, there's a whole lot I've missed about Banks over all the years I was too busy trying to ignore my crush on him.

"Only my therapist knows all the details." His fingers trail up and down my arm, leaving goosebumps in their wake. "And now you."

Something shifts between us with that admission. He's

letting me see this piece of himself that he keeps hidden from everyone else, and it makes my chest tight, and an entire kaleidoscope of butterflies take flight in my stomach.

"I sleep better too," I whisper, feeling the need to give him something for the gift he's just given me. "I used to lie awake for hours in this creaky old building, jumping at every single sound." I force myself to keep my eyes locked on his so he'll see the truth in my words. "Now I just... I know you're there. On the other side of the wall."

His arm pulls me tighter against him until my cheek is pressed against his chest and he presses a kiss to the top of my head. His steady heartbeat's thumping against my ear while my own is going completely haywire.

Lightning flashes again, and the room lights up in brief, stark white. In that split second, I see the intense look in his eyes as he stares down at me. It's feral and predatory and *oh my fucking god* so hot.

"This is because of the storm, right?" I murmur, needing to blame the way I'm about to fold like a cheap card table on something. "Because it's dark and loud and we're trapped?"

"Sure," he agrees but his voice is rough, and his fingers tighten where they're pressed into my skin.

I think it's clear we're both liars.

The lightning and thunder decide to hit at the exact same time, booming so loud it feels like the windows are going to shatter in their frames. I jump, letting out this pathetic little squeak of a sound, and burrow even closer to him.

His arms tighten around me, one hand sliding up to grip the back of my neck, his fingers threading through my hair. It's possessive, the way his rough fingers tighten against my skin.

"I've got you," he murmurs, his lips brushing against my temple. "Nothing's going to hurt you as long as I'm breathing."

I tilt my head back because my feminism's got her protest signs all ready to go, but the words die in my throat the second I see his face in the flickering candlelight. His eyes are dark, almost black and locked onto me. I could count every single one of his long eyelashes if I wanted to. I can see the tiny, almost invisible scar cutting through his left eyebrow, notice the stubble starting to darken his jaw even though I know he shaved this morning.

"Banks," I breathe out, his name sounding more like a question than anything else. Or maybe it's an invitation.

He answers by slowly sliding his other hand up to my face, his thumb brushing back and forth over my bottom lip. The feather-light touch makes me tremble all the way down to my toes. When his eyes drop to my mouth, the raw, undisguised hunger burning there sets my body on fire.

"Tell me to stop, Clover," he whispers, his voice so deep and rough it barely even sounds like him.

I absolutely should. Every logical, rational part of my brain is screaming at me to stop this right now. He's my brother's best friend. Giving in would complicate absolutely everything in ways I can't even begin to comprehend.

But logic doesn't stand a single goddamn chance against the way he's looking at my mouth like he'll actually die if he doesn't get to taste it. Against the heat of his fingers curled around my neck and pressing into my skin. Against all the years I've spent pretending I haven't been dreaming of exactly this.

So, I answer him by closing the last little bit of distance between us and finally, *finally* kissing him.

He freezes for one heart-stopping second, and I start to spiral. Did I just make a monumental, life-altering mistake? Then he makes this guttural sound—half groan, half growl—that vibrates deep in his chest and up through my body, setting off a whole new wave of heat. His mouth crashes down on mine again, any hesitation long gone as the kiss turns feral. Wild. Desperate.

I gasp, and he takes immediate advantage, deepening the

kiss as his fingers tangle in my hair, gripping almost painfully. He kisses like he's been starving for a taste of me, like he's trying to memorize every single sound I make and the way his mouth fits against mine.

And I surrender to my craving for him. Let loose the curiosity I've held back for years. Sink into his hold on me and the way his tongue tastes as it slides against mine.

The storm raging outside has absolutely nothing on the one that just broke loose in here between us. It's a hurricane unleashed, and we're both being swept away.

11
Clover

I'VE HAD my fair share of kisses. But nothing—absolutely nothing—could have prepared me for being kissed by my brother's best friend. He doesn't just kiss me; he consumes me. It's like he can't get enough as his teeth nip at my bottom lip, sucking it into his mouth. He's writing his name on my soul with every stroke of his tongue, every scrape of his stubble against my skin, every shift of his fingers tightening on the back of my neck, holding me prisoner to what's happening between us.

In all my fantasies about kissing my brother's best friend, I never could've imagined *this*.

The muscles in his arms flex as he drags me onto his lap, and I make a sound I didn't even know I was capable of making when I feel how hard he is for me.

"Fuck, Clover," he groans and that sound—god, that fucking sound. I want to live in that sound. Wrap it around myself like a blanket.

My entire body shudders.

I want to beg him to touch me everywhere. To let those big, calloused hands of his run all over my body. To touch him, explore the miles of inked skin and hard muscle. But I can't seem to form the words, and I don't need to. Because when he lifts his hips and presses that impressive length right against where I'm dying to feel it, it's like he knows. Like he can read every thought in my head.

Lightning flashes again, throwing us into nearly blinding white light for a split second. His eyes are wild, pupils completely blown, looking up at me like I'm the only thing he's ever wanted in his entire life.

I slide my hands up his chest, feeling his rapid heartbeat under my palms. His skin feels like it's on fire, his muscles rock hard and flexed tight. I have the briefest urge to pinch myself because there's absolutely no way this is actually happening.

Banks Priestly is looking at me like I'm all his fucking dreams come true.

He grips my hips and grinds up into me, pulling a moan from somewhere so deep it feels like it's being ripped right out of my soul. That sound coming from me makes him pull in a sharp breath, his grip tightening to an almost bruising intensity. The pain mingles with the pleasure and it's so good, too good, and I want more.

He tears his mouth from mine and drags it down the curve of my neck, his lips and teeth scraping over my sensitive skin. My hands find their way into his hair, fingers gripping and tugging every time he rolls his hips up into mine. I can barely catch my breath, everything inside of me tightening as his mouth works miracles against my skin.

His teeth graze against the curve of my shoulder, biting down just enough to sting. "You have no idea how long I've wanted this," he says, his lips brushing against the sting from his bite with his words.

"How long?"

My breath catches in my throat as his lips and tongue and teeth work a trail of fire back up the side of my neck. He's leaving his mark everywhere he touches, and I don't think it's only my skin that will bear the reminders of tonight as I dig my nails into his shoulders.

"I want you so bad, I can hardly breathe," he whispers, his lips brushing against the shell of my ear. "You're all I think about. You're all I dream about. You've been driving me insane for years."

I'm not sure if he realizes what he just admitted, but it makes me feel bold. Wanted. Sexy.

"Tell me you want this," he demands as his fingers dig into my hips hard enough to bruise. He's leaving marks all over my skin like he needs to know neither one of us can deny what's happening.

"I want this," I tell him, rolling my hips and rubbing against that thick, hard dick of his I can't wait to get my hands on. My pussy is so wet for him, I can feel it soaking through the fabric of my underwear. His hands grip my ass and he stands, stumbling a bit because his mouth is back on mine and we're rubbing all over each other so much neither of us can bear to let the other one go.

He knocks the lamp off the end table, and it crashes to the ground but we don't stop. His tongue is in my mouth, his hands are on my ass and my back slams up against the wall. My legs are wrapped around him and he's grinding into me, my body jerking and writhing against the wall. I'm pretty sure he's going to make me come just by dry humping.

"God, I need to be inside of you," he groans, as I let go of him long enough to rip my shirt over my head and he reaches behind his neck and does the same, gripping his shirt and yanking it over his head. I'm not wearing a bra and the way his eyes go wide when he looks at me, the way his nostrils flare and his gaze darkens, makes me feel sexier than I ever have. It's like I'm a goddess and he's my most devoted worshipper.

I'm going to let Banks Priestly fuck me tonight and I don't think I've ever been more excited about anything in my life.

"So get inside of me."

"Fuck," he bites out, reaching between us to tear open the button on his jeans while he drops one of my legs so I can shimmy one leg out of my shorts and underwear. The need to get naked is urgent, but I can't wait long enough to get completely undressed.

I want him and I want him now.

I've never wanted anything this much in my whole entire life. I'm shaking, I'm trembling, my heart is racing, my pulse pounding. Everything in me is screaming for him and I can't hold back anymore.

He pulls his dick out of his jeans and I don't get any time to appreciate the sight because he has my leg back in the air and he's pressing against me. He grips the base of it, rubs it against my wet pussy, and then he thrusts. One solid, quick, hard stroke that drives the entire length of him inside of me in one motion. I gasp at the feeling, the sensation of being filled by him. He's so big and I'm so wet. It's perfect.

He's perfect.

"Oh my god," I whisper, resting my forehead against his, my entire body clenching and tightening around him. "Banks, oh my god."

"Fuck, baby, fuck." He thrusts into me, pulling almost all the way out before plunging back inside. Over and over again. His pace is hard, fast, rough, relentless. His fingers dig into my ass as he pulls my body into his with each drive of his hips like he can't get deep enough inside of me.

He's still inside me as he kicks off his pants and boxer briefs, stumbling away from the wall. His arms shake as we move. He's fucking me as he walks toward my bedroom, and I can't even believe the strength in him. Can't even fathom the power in his body. He carries me, fucking into me with every step until he curses. "Fuck, I'm going to come."

Yes, yes, fuck yes. I want that.

My arms are around wrapped around his neck and I use my hold on him to lift myself up and fuck myself back down on him so he can't hold back. He stops halfway down the hall and his head falls back while he lets out the hottest groan I've ever heard as he comes. His legs shake and the muscles in his chest, arms, and neck strain while his cock pulses.

"Fuck, I'm sorry," he moans as he empties himself inside of me. His voice is rough and so fucking sexy. "Fuck, fuck, fuck, I'm sorry."

"God, that was hot," I tell him as his cock twitches inside me. It's still hard and when he finally takes a step toward the bedroom again, he hits something deep inside of me that makes my entire body shudder.

"Yeah? I've never come that fast, but you... fuck, I couldn't help myself. You drive me fucking crazy." He drops his forehead to mine. "I'll make it up to you."

His elbow slams against the doorframe as he carries me into my bedroom, and he grunts. But he doesn't lose his grip on me, and he doesn't pull out of me either. Instead, he walks across the room and lays me out on the bed like I'm a precious gift. The way he looks at me is almost reverent as his eyes rake over my body stop between my thighs. His hand slides up the back of my leg, and he yanks my shorts off and tosses them over his shoulder before he pulls it up to sit on his shoulder, kissing my calf as he stares down at where his dick is still inside of me.

"Look at you, taking my dick so well," he murmurs, his eyes glued between my legs. The sound of his voice makes my pussy clench around him and his jaw tics. "God damn."

He bends my leg back, opening my body to him even more, and starts to move. Slowly. He's watching where he's fucking me, where he's sliding in and out of me. And then his fingers are against my clit. Everything's slippery and wet and he's sliding right against it, rubbing me in rhythm with the slow rolls of his hips.

How is he still hard?

"I love seeing you full of my dick," he tells me. "Knowing how deep inside of you I am."

I whimper. My body's climbing higher and higher as he works me over. As he grinds into me, making sure to rub that big, hard dick of his against my g-spot with every lazy roll of his hips. I can't even hear the storm outside with the way my heart is pounding. My skin is slick with sweat and my breath is coming in shallow, panting gasps as I get closer and closer to the edge.

"Look at me," he commands, and I open my eyes. He's looking down at me like nothing else in the world matters except the two of us. The look in his eyes is savage. Rabid. It's a look that's meant to claim, to own, to mark. "I'm going to spend all night making your pretty pussy come. Teaching it who owns it now."

Oh, god.

He pinches my clit, and I cry out, my body clenching and spasming as I come. Hard. So hard, I see stars. It's like I'm being sucked into a black hole, and I can't do anything but fall. My entire body shakes, trembles, quakes as the orgasm rips through me. His fingers and his cock are relentless, stealing every bit of pleasure he can from me.

"God, you're fucking beautiful," he says as he leans over me and crushes his mouth to mine. I wrap myself around him, holding onto him like I'm about to float away. And it's a good thing I do because he rolls, taking me with him until he's flat on his back and I'm straddling him. Our bodies are still joined together, and he's still so hard, it makes no sense.

"Banks," I gasp as his cock shifts inside of me, hitting me in places I didn't even know existed.

He smiles at me. A wicked, sinful, toe-curling smile that makes his eyes glitter in the dark. And then his fingers tighten on my hips, and he uses them to lift my body off his dick. I slide up until just the tip is inside of me and then he yanks me back down. My head falls back, and my hair tickles the small of my back as he uses my body like a toy. He's grinning as he fucks into me, and I don't ever want to stop.

"Play with your tits," he says, and I do. I cup my breasts and tweak my nipples, rolling the stiff peaks between my fingers. It makes my pussy tighten around him, and his thrusts grow more frantic. "God, that's so fucking hot."

Nothing has ever felt better than having Banks Priestly between my legs, looking up at me like he's the one who's never felt anything better than being inside of me.

I drop forward and kiss him. Our tongues and teeth clash as he drives up into me, fucking me from below. It feels incredible. I want it to last forever. And yet...

"Banks," I moan his name as I come again, tightening around him while his pelvis rubs against my clit at the perfect angle. "Fill me again. Please. I need it. Need to feel it."

"Fuck," he groans as he thrusts into me again, then one last time, his entire body going stiff as he shoots hot and deep inside of me. I can feel every twitch of his dick as it spasms and jerks. Every pulse as he fills me. "God, yes, take my cum. Take all of it. Every fucking drop of it."

He rolls us again, putting me on my back as he settles on top of me, his hips grinding into mine as his cock keeps pumping cum inside of me. My arms are around his neck, and I hold on to him as he rides out the wave, as his body jerks and shudders. His face is buried in the crook of my neck, and I feel the heat of his breath against my skin.

"Damn," he murmurs, his lips pressing a kiss against my neck. "I've never come so hard in my entire life."

"Me either," I tell him.

He lifts his head, pushing up on his elbows to look down at me. "Yeah?"

I nod and bite my lip to hide the smile trying to break out over it. I don't know what it is about the awe in his voice that makes me want to giggle, but I'm not about to let him hear that right now.

He kisses my forehead. Then my nose. And finally, my mouth. It's soft and sweet and I can feel his smile as he does it. When he pulls away, he brushes my hair back off my cheek and then pulls me down so I'm cuddled up against him.

For a long time, neither of us speaks. There's just the sound of our breathing gradually starting to even out and the distant rumble of thunder as the storm slowly starts to move on.

Banks's fingers run through my hair and I sigh, letting my heavy eyes close. I'm tucked against Banks's body like he can't stand the thought of even a sliver of space existing between us.

I really should be freaking the hell out right now. Panicking about what we just did and all the catastrophic ways this could potentially blow up in both of our faces. But as I lie here, with Banks's steady heartbeat thumping under my palm, all I feel is this unexpected sense of peace that I can't remember ever feeling before.

"You good, Freckles?" he asks, his fingers tracing these slow, lazy circles on my bare back now.

"I'm..." I search for the right word and finally just settle on the truth. "Yeah. Actually, really good." I trace the lines of one of the tattoos on his chest. "That was..."

"Mind-blowing?" he offers, a hint of his usual cockiness in his voice.

I nod against his chest, not having the energy to look for better words to describe what just happened between us. We fall quiet again, just breathing together as the storm rumbles off in the distance. He's different like this—softer somehow, all that usual cockiness gone. And honestly? I kind of really like seeing him this way.

"We should probably actually talk about what just happened," I finally say, because someone has to be the responsible adult in this situation, and that unfortunate job always falls to me. Sometimes I really hate being this person.

"Probably," he agrees, but his arms just tighten around me, pulling me even closer. "Or... we could just enjoy this for another minute before reality ruins everything."

Maybe it's smarter to have "the talk" right now, get all the awkwardness and consequences out of the way. But I just can't bring myself to ruin this moment with all the reasons we shouldn't have done what we just did. That conversation makes me unfathomably sad and feels way too heavy for my exhausted body to handle at the moment.

Instead, I just curl even closer to him, my head finding that perfect little spot right on his chest where I can clearly hear his steady heartbeat. His arms wrap tighter around me, like they were divinely designed to hold me exactly like this.

"We'll figure it out tomorrow," I murmur sleepily, my eyelids already slipping shut.

"Whatever you want, Freckles." He presses another soft kiss to the top of my head. "I'll be right here."

As I start to drift off, that annoying little voice of reality tries to creep in, whispering all sorts of unwelcome reminders: We've officially crossed a line that can never be uncrossed. Everything between us is different now. Kasen might murder Banks when he eventually finds out what just happened. And he may never speak to me again.

But with Banks's heartbeat thumping under my ear and his arms locked tight around me like he's afraid I might disappear if he lets go, I let myself believe that maybe this doesn't have to be just some temporary, heat-of-the-moment thing.

Maybe it could actually be so much more.

I wake up to sunlight assaulting me through my thin curtains. *Guess the storm's over.* I'm about to roll over and bury my face in the pillow when I become very, very aware of several things all at once: the heavy weight of an arm slung possessively around my waist, the warmth of another body pressed against my back, and the delicious ache between my thighs.

Oh damn.

Last night comes flooding back in a rush of toe-curling detail. The storm. The blackout. The life-altering kiss. Being fucked up against the wall. Banks ruining me in this bed. The filthy, delicious things he whispered in the dark while he made me come undone.

Holy freaking hell. I had sex with Banks Priestly.

Well, it's official. My brother is one hundred percent going to murder me. Probably Banks, too, if Kasen gets to him first.

I turn over as carefully as humanly possible, trying not to wake him, but his eyes are already open. Those hazel eyes that saw every single inch of me last night, that now know exactly what I look like naked and begging him to make me come, are currently studying my face with the same unwavering attention he always gives me.

"Morning," he says, his voice a low, husky rumble that sends a fresh wave of goosebumps skittering across my skin from the tips of my toes all the way to the top of my head. Ugh, I am in *so* much trouble.

"Hi," I manage to squeak out. Why the hell do I sound so breathless? I clear my throat and quickly glance around my bedroom, noticing the flashing numbers on my alarm clock. "Looks like the power's back on."

This is so awkward.

"Yeah," he agrees softly, his thumb drawing slow, lazy circles on my bare hip under the sheet, and it feels way, way too good. "Sleep okay?"

"Better than I have in..." *Forever.* "A while."

Something hot flashes in his eyes, a brief flicker of something intense and maybe even a little possessive, before his expression smooths out, becoming more guarded. "About last night..."

And here we go. The awkward morning-after conversation where we both pretend it was just some moment of temporary insanity brought on by the storm and the close proximity. Where we agree to never speak of it again and try our very best to avoid making direct eye contact for the rest of the time we're stuck living together.

I need to say it first, before he does. Rip off the damn band-aid and all that.

"It was the storm," I blurt out, the words tumbling out way too fast. "And the power outage. And being stuck here together in the dark. Just... a mistake." The words taste like ash in my mouth as I say them. I *hate* that I'm saying them. I want to grab them and shove them back in even as more pop out. "A onetime thing that doesn't have to make things weird or change anything."

Liar, liar, my entire damn body is currently on fire.

Something in his face closes off, and his thumb stops its lazy circles against my hip, but he just gives this small, tight nod. "Right. A mistake."

His easy agreement shouldn't feel like a baseball bat to the chest, but it absolutely does.

"We're adults," I continue, even as this hollow, sinking feeling starts to spread through my chest. "We can admit that things got a little intense last night, but we can also agree that it probably shouldn't happen again."

His eyes narrow. "Shouldn't," he repeats slowly, his gaze intense. "Or... can't?"

The question just hangs there between us. "Both," I finally manage to choke out, ignoring the way every single cell in my body is screaming at me to shut the hell up.

Why am I even doing this again?

Oh, right. My overprotective brother. And my very specific life goals. And the fact that Banks is exactly the type of guy to sleep with a woman and be gone before the sun even thinks about rising.

There are a million perfectly logical reasons, but they all feel flimsy and unimportant right now when all I really want to do is reach out and hold on to him. "You're Kasen's best friend. I'm his little sister. We're temporary roommates. You only do casual, and I don't exactly have the time or the inclination for anything complicated. It would be a disaster."

His eyes roam over my face for what feels like an eternity, like he's searching for something. I hold my breath, waiting. Finally, he nods once, his jaw clenching. "Sure. It's not a big deal. Nothing needs to change."

I should feel relieved. This is exactly what I wanted him to say, right? So why does it feel like he just reached into my chest and crushed something vital?

I'm the one who called what we did a mistake in the first place, so why the hell are my eyes stinging like I'm about to cry?

"Great," I say, forcing a bright, cheerful smile that feels like it might crack my face in half. "So... we're good then?"

"We're good," he agrees, and the smile he gives me in return doesn't even come anywhere close to reaching his eyes. Then he leans forward and presses a quick, soft kiss to my forehead that somehow manages to hurt way worse than if he'd just slapped me across the face. "I should probably go take a shower."

He slides out of bed, and I watch every single ripple of muscle in his back as he stretches. I really shouldn't look. It's only going to make this whole thing even harder. But I can't seem to tear my eyes away from the man who completely and utterly wrecked me just a few short hours ago.

I swallow hard, fighting back the tears that are threatening to spill over. I'm starting to have this awful feeling that he might have just ruined me for anyone else.

At the door, he stops and turns back. The raw, honest expression on his face makes my breath catch in my throat—it's something that wasn't there even just a minute ago when we were both lying our asses off to each other.

"For what it's worth, Freckles," he says, his voice low and rough, like he hasn't quite cleared the sleep from it yet, "last night was the best damn mistake I've ever made in my entire life. And I wouldn't take back a single fucking second of it."

Then he's gone, and I'm left alone in my bedroom with wrinkled sheets that still smell like him and the feeling that we just made everything a thousand times more complicated by pretending last night wasn't everything.

Because no matter what kind of bullshit we just fed each other, I know—I absolutely know—that nothing between us will ever, ever be the same again.

And the only thing that might be worse than knowing it was a terrible idea?

Wanting to do it all over again.

12
Banks

A MONTH IS a long goddamn time to pretend you're not crawling out of your skin for someone who sleeps less than fifty feet away.

That you're not completely fucked up and obsessed.

Thirty-three fucking days since that night in the middle of the storm. Thirty-three days of Clover breezing around in tiny sleep shorts, daring me not to picture ripping them off. Thirty-three days of casual brushes in the hall that set my nerves on fire. Thirty-three days of replaying exactly how she tastes, how she sounds when she comes, how perfectly she fit around me.

And thirty-three days of acting like it never happened.

"Priestly!" Captain Morgan's bark slices through my memories like a buzz saw. "Quit daydreaming and get your ass back on the platform!"

I blink, realizing I'm dangling twenty feet above the training yard, harnessed up like a Christmas ornament. The rescue dummy sways below me on the rope I'm supposed to be controlling. Instead, I've been busy picturing Clover's fingernails raking down my back.

"Shit. Sorry, Cap!" I yank the line to continue the exercise.

Morgan's face is a storm cloud. He doesn't even need to shout—his silent disappointment is worse than any curse he could hurl. Around us, the rest of the crew suddenly finds their own gear fascinating, desperate not to be the next one in his crosshairs.

Ten minutes later, I'm back in his office, standing at attention while he tears me a new asshole. I stare at the wall behind him, trying not to wilt under his glare.

"Third time this week, Priestly. Third. Fucking. Time." Morgan's eyebrows have fused into one giant caterpillar of rage. "What the hell's going on inside that thick skull of yours? You keep this up, someone's gonna die."

I square my shoulders. "No excuses, sir. It won't happen again."

Morgan scowls. "It damn well better not. This isn't a joke. I've got five other guys counting on you to be fully present, and your head's off in la-la land. Get it together or enjoy desk duty."

My stomach twists. Not because this is new—he's chewed me out before—but because I know he's right. My dad died because his partner lost focus on a routine call. One second of drifting can cost everything. If anyone should remember that, it's me.

"I understand, sir."

He leans forward, eyes narrowed. "This about that girl you're shacking up with? Your buddy's sister?"

My jaw grits. The fact he even remembers that conversation from a month ago catches me off guard. "What makes you think that?"

"Twenty years in this job, kid. I can tell when a man's mind is somewhere else. And yours is clearly stuck on her."

A lump forms in my throat. Denying it is useless—Morgan sees right through me. "Yeah. Something like that. It's... complicated."

"You said that last time we talked. Maybe it's time you

uncomplicate it." He stands, effectively ending the discussion. "Fix your shit or I'm benching you indefinitely. I won't have my crew put at risk because you can't keep your dick in your pants."

Am I really that fucking transparent?

It's a goddamn miracle Kasen hasn't figured me out yet.

I storm out of his office and head straight to the locker room, needing a breather to get my head on straight. I fling my locker open, the metal door cracking against the next one with a clang.

"Wow. Looks like someone's having a stellar day."

I whirl around. Brenna's leaning in the doorway, arms crossed. Her blonde curls are pulled back in a tight braid, and she's wearing the kind of expression that says she knows exactly what's got me so pissed I could punch a hole in the wall.

"Not now, Foxton."

"Oh, we're doing this right now." She steps inside, completely unbothered by my warning tone. "You almost dropped a rescue dummy from twenty feet up. That's a kid, a victim, or one of us in a real scenario."

My hands drag through my hair, tugging hard enough to hurt. "I fucking know that."

"Then act like it." She moves closer, voice dropping. "You've been half-dead for weeks. Today you nearly botched a rescue drill. Tomorrow it might be the real thing." Her gaze drills into me. "It's about her, right? Clover?"

I groan. "Morgan just ripped me a new one. I don't need you piling on. You're supposed to be my friend."

"I am," she snaps. "That's why I'm calling you out. You're a mess over this girl."

A fresh wave of anger—and embarrassment—surges through me. "Why does everyone think my entire life revolves around that woman?" I slam the locker shut, the echo reverberating through the empty room.

"Because you're walking around looking like my little brother after his first girlfriend dumped him—like somebody just curb-stomped your puppy, stole your ice cream, and told you Santa isn't real all at once." Brenna sinks onto the bench, clearly not leaving until she gets answers. "So? Did you sleep with the bartender or not?"

My anger deflates in a single whoosh. I slump onto the bench, suddenly exhausted. "Yes."

"And?"

"And now we're pretending it never happened." I press the heels of my hands to my temples, trying to stave off the headache that's been brewing all day. "It was her call, not mine."

Brenna lets out a low whistle. "That good, huh?"

"You have no idea." The memory blindsides me again—Clover beneath me, eyes locked on mine, saying my name like it meant everything. "It was... fuck, Bren. It was everything."

"So what's stopping you from going for it?" She narrows her eyes, then answers her own question. "Her brother, obviously."

"That's part of it." I recall that morning after—Clover fortifying her walls, brick by stubborn brick, right in front of me. "She said it was a mistake. Because she's Kasen's sister, and I 'only do casual.'" I practically spit the words, disgust rolling in my gut.

Brenna arches a brow. "Well, you have been the dictionary definition of a fuckboy ever since I met you."

"Yeah, well..." I stare at my hands, remembering how they felt on Clover's skin. "It's what everyone expects from me." *Or wants me for.*

"Bullshit."

I look up, thrown by the sudden edge in Brenna's voice.

"That's total bullshit, Banks." She crosses her arms and fixes me with a hard stare. "You're the guy who brings soup to Vetter's kids when they're sick. Who spent a weekend moving

Martinez's grandma into her new apartment. Who volunteers at the burn unit on your days off."

"That's different."

"Is it?" She bumps my shoulder with hers. "Or have you just gotten so used to people treating you like you're only good for a one-night stand that you forgot who you really are?" She shakes her head. "Women like Clover need somebody who shows up. Someone who stays when it gets ugly. And guess what—lucky her, that's the guy you actually are."

Her words hit me like a lightning bolt. Is that what Clover needs—someone who proves he's here for the long haul, not another hookup who vanishes when things get complicated?

Does she need to see that I'm willing to put her before my best friend?

"Look," Brenna goes on, pushing to her feet. "I don't know exactly what's up with you two, but ever since that 'whatever happened,' you haven't been yourself. So either tell her how you feel or walk away, because this half-in, half-out shit is dangerous. For you, and for the rest of us." She squeezes my shoulder. "Figure it out before Morgan benches your ass. I can't deal with Johnson as a rescue partner. The jackass still calls me 'little lady.'"

She heads out, and I'm left sitting there, her words rattling around in my head.

The problem is I've been waiting in the wings for Clover James since the first time I saw her across Kasen's living room, but I never believed I had a shot.

Now I know she wants me too, except she's shutting me out.

⛈

The automatic doors whoosh open as I enter the grocery store, cold AC blasting across my face. It's my day off, and I'm on a mission to cook something for dinner that might coax Clover into eating with me instead of working late at Ember again.

For the past week, she's been sneaking in after I'm out cold and slipping away before I'm up. I'd think she was flat out dodging me, except she keeps leaving little things in the fridge with my name on them. Like she's trying to take care of me while still keeping me at arm's length.

It's driving me fucking insane.

I'm standing in the meat section, debating between steak or the salmon Clover mentioned liking a while back, when I hear a familiar voice.

"Banks? Is that you?"

I turn to find Haley Price standing there, looking exactly like she did when we dated three years ago. Her hair's perfect, her clothes are too expensive for grocery shopping, and her smile's just this side of crazy.

"Haley." I nod, already trying to figure out how to get the hell out of here. "How are you?"

"I'm wonderful." She steps closer, her hand sliding up my arm like she has the right to touch me. I shake her off without being a dick about it, adjusting the basket I'm carrying to make the move seem natural. "It's been forever. We should catch up sometime."

The way she says "catch up" makes it clear she's not thinking about getting coffee.

Six months ago—even three months ago—I might've considered it. Haley and I were good at no-strings sex. She never asked for more than I was willing to give, and I never had to worry about hurting her.

But now? I feel absolutely nothing as she gives me a look that's trying too hard to be tempting. I'm not into it. Her touch feels wrong. She doesn't have freckles on her nose, and she's not gonna give me shit for swapping where the forks and spoons go in the silverware drawer just to piss her off.

She's not Clover.

"I'm seeing home." It's a lie that feels like the truth. Because in my head, I *am* seeing someone. Doesn't matter that Clover and I aren't actually together. I'm all in, whether she is or not.

Maybe she's not seeing me, but I'm sure as fuck seeing her.

Haley's eyes narrow and the flirty smile drops off her face. "Anyone I know?"

"I doubt it." I take another step back and turn toward the produce so she gets the message. "Good seeing you, Haley. Take care."

I'm gone before she can try another angle, grabbing fresh dill and a lemon on the way to the checkout. With a clearer head than I've had in days, I realize I'm done letting Clover steer this situation. Brenna said it herself: show up. So that's what I'm doing.

I pay for my groceries and my plan churns in my mind all the way home. Enough pretending. Enough letting Clover decide every rule. She's got this idea that it meant nothing, or that I'm not the guy who can handle more. She's wrong.

It's time to stop lying to myself. To her. To everyone.

The apartment's quiet when I step inside—no shock there. She's supposed to be at class for another hour. But then I hear a retching noise coming from the bathroom.

"Clover?" I set the grocery bags on the counter, heart pounding. "You okay?"

A fresh wave of gagging is my only answer. I hurry to the bathroom and push open the door.

She's on her knees, hugging the toilet, hair stuck to her forehead. Sweat glistens on her pale cheeks. She looks miserable as hell.

"Get out!" she chokes, voice cracking between heaves. "I don't...want you seeing me like this."

I ignore her, kneeling beside her anyway. I scoop her hair

off her face with one hand and rub her back with the other, letting her throw up again.

"It's okay," I say quietly, keeping my voice steady. "I've got you."

Seeing her so vulnerable rips a hole right through my chest. My pulse is thrashing, and my hands shake as I do the only thing I can—offer support.

She tries feebly to push me away, but another round of nausea hits and she doubles over. I hold her hair and keep my hand moving in slow circles across her spine, helpless anger and worry tangling in my gut.

Finally, she sags against the toilet, exhausted. I flush away the evidence, then stand to wet a washcloth with cool water. Dropping back to my knees, I press it to her forehead, fighting the urge to gather her in my arms.

"What are you doing?" she whispers, eyes scrunched shut.

"Taking care of you." My thumb skims across her cheek, brushing a stray strand of hair aside. "How long's this been going on?"

"Started during class," she admits, eyes squeezing shut at another wave of nausea. She leans into the cool cloth I'm pressing against her forehead, but it's like she hates needing it. "I figured I'd get home and ride it out before you got back."

"So I wouldn't see you like this?" I can't keep the hurt from creeping into my voice. "Clover, I don't care if you're puking your guts out—I care that you're sick."

She opens her eyes, and the raw vulnerability there twists a knife in my chest. "I hate being weak."

"Being sick isn't weak; it's human." Gently, I guide her upright, my arm steadying her when her legs wobble. She gives in, leaning against me. "Come on, rinse your mouth, then we'll get you on the couch."

She must feel like absolute hell, because she doesn't argue. Five minutes later, she's tucked under a blanket, a mixing bowl nearby just in case. I'm in the kitchen heating water for ginger tea and rummaging up saltines like my mom used to give me when I had a stomach bug as a kid. The memory makes me smile; I haven't thought about it in years.

When I come back, she's curled in on herself, looking a little pathetic. Something inside my chest tightens at the sight, this fierce protectiveness and possessiveness knot together with everything else I feel for her.

"Here." I set the tea and crackers on the coffee table, then sit beside her. "Ginger should help your stomach."

She blinks up at me, eyes glassy. "Why...why are you doing this?"

"What do you mean?"

"Taking care of me. You don't have to." She tries to sit up, and I immediately slip an arm behind her shoulders, supporting her. "I'm not asking you to, okay? I don't need—"

Her words cut, but I push past it. Tonight's obviously not the time to lay out all the feelings I've been obsessing over, but I can give her something. "Maybe I need to, ever think of that?"

She stares, clearly thrown by my honesty.

"Drink," I say quietly, pressing the mug into her hands. "Small sips."

For once she listens, and that's how I know she must feel like shit. She watches me over the rim of the mug, her expression impossible to read. After a few careful swallows, she sets it down and sinks into the cushions, exhaustion radiating from every line of her body.

"I'm supposed to work tonight," she mutters. "I need to call Navy."

"Already done." I pull out my phone, waving it slightly. "I texted her while the water was boiling. She says don't worry about the bar—just get better."

Clover glares at me with a mix of annoyance and reluctant gratitude. "So you just took over my life, huh?"

"Yep. But I promise I'll give it back as soon as you're on your feet." Maybe. I can't resist a small grin. "And don't act like you wouldn't do the same for me."

She tries to muster some sass. "Would I?" But there's no real bite behind the words.

"Yeah, you would." I brush her hair back from her face, letting my fingers linger longer than strictly necessary. "You act all tough, but you've got the biggest heart of anyone I know, Freckles."

She doesn't snap at the nickname, and that says everything about how lousy she feels.

We sit in silence for a while, the only sounds are her occasional sips of tea and my phone buzzing with texts from Kasen asking about the Blazers game tomorrow night. I ignore it. Nothing else matters right now except the woman in front of me.

It doesn't take long for the drowsiness to win out—her eyelids droop, and she shifts, pressing her head against my chest like she isn't even aware she's doing it. "Just until I feel better," she whispers, voice barely audible. Her body settles into mine, fitting so well it's like we're two pieces of a puzzle snapping into place.

I slide an arm around her, stroking her hair. "Take all the time you need."

She's out in minutes. I watch her breathe, every rise and fall of her shoulders, the way her lashes rest on her cheeks. The constellation of freckles dusting her nose are mesmerizing, and I realize I'm grinning like an idiot.

"I'm exactly where I want to be," I murmur into her hair, letting the words free because she can't hear them. But I swear there's a tiny smile that tugs at the corner of her mouth, like some part of her does.

Time slips by, my arm dead asleep beneath her. My back starts to twinge, but I don't move. I'd sit here forever if she needed me to. Eventually, though, practical concerns—like my spine—force me to shift. Carefully, I slide an arm under her knees and another around her back, lifting her against my chest. She mumbles something and nestles closer, her fingers twisting in my shirt while I carry her into her room.

She clutches my sleeve even when I lay her down, and for a second, I consider leaving. I know she's spent the last month enforcing walls between us. But she's not letting go, and the truth is, I don't want to leave. So I sit on the edge of her bed, running my fingertips through her hair and across her forehead, memorizing the curve of her cheek, the shape of her lips, the freckles I'd never be allowed to get close enough to study if she were awake.

"When did you start feeling like home?" I murmur, the question hanging between us in the quiet. I'm not sure when it happened—when she went from being my best friend's sister to the center of my goddamn world. When her independence became the thing I respect the most, when her walls became something I want to climb and then guard instead of break down.

All I know is that somewhere between that first morning making coffee in her kitchen and tonight, watching her sleep, denial transformed into something that feels an awful lot like forever.

I force myself upright before I do something I can't take back, like crawl in beside her and show her exactly how I feel. Standing in the doorway, I drink in the sight of her one more time—the woman I want, in the space we share but don't really share, with the life she's built that I'd give anything to be part of.

Casual, my ass. Nothing about my feelings for Clover James is casual. And I'll prove it to her... one way or another.

13
Clover

FUCK.

I'm so fucking fucked.

I blink. Stare down at it harder. Blink again. Swear I'll never complain about anything ever again if this *one thing* goes how I need it to.

Yeah, no.

There are still two pink lines on the fucking *pregnancy test* clutched in my hands.

This can't be happening.

I refuse.

It *cannot*.

I set the pregnancy test on the bathroom counter with fingers that won't stop shaking and grip the edge of the sink to keep myself from just keeling over because I can't life anymore. The white-knuckle hold I have on the porcelain is the only thing keeping me upright right now.

"Shit. Shit. *Shit*." I mutter to my reflection like it's her fault instead of mine we're in this situation.

But joke's on me—there's no one to blame but this idiot right here.

I'm pregnant. *With Banks Priestly's baby.*

Honestly?

I don't even know how to *begin* to process this.

Banks. My temporary roommate. My brother's *hotter than anyone I've ever met and has real life abs* best friend. The guy who whispered all those dirty words with his mouth on my skin six weeks ago. Of course then I pushed him away because I'm an asshole and couldn't cope with the consequences of what we did or how it made me feel.

I've regretted it for the last six weeks and now the joke's on me. I've got enough consequences to deal with to literally last a lifetime and not a single shoulder to cry on.

I sink down to the floor as I do something I haven't let myself do in six weeks—I think back to that night. The one where we couldn't keep our hands off each other long enough to think about basic protection.

Ugh. How could we be so stupid?

I close my eyes but that just makes it worse because now I'm seeing it all in crystal fucking clear high def—Banks pinning me to the wall, his teeth scraping along my neck, marking me. The way we practically tore each other's clothes off. His voice all gravelly in my ear, telling me how he's *wanted this for so long, Freckles* while he pushed inside me. The way I wrapped my legs around him, pulling him deeper, begging for *more more more* while neither of us even breathed the word "condom" because we were too busy drowning in each other.

And now here I am. Sitting on my bathroom floor staring at the result of that night. Two pink lines that are about to change everything.

The nausea that's been kicking my ass for two weeks rolls through me again. I've been lying to myself—telling myself it was stress or maybe food poisoning or literally anything other than what it obviously is. But the missed period? Boobs that hurt so bad even breathing makes them ache? I'm an idiot for not connecting the dots sooner.

No one can know about this. Not until I figure out what the hell I'm going to do. Not until I work out how to tell Banks that our "onetime mistake" just turned into the most permanent thing either of us will ever do.

"Stupid hot alphahole firefighter," I mutter to Bellini, the jade plant that lives on the bathroom windowsill. "This is his fault for being so irresistible. I blame him."

My phone buzzes, and I see text pop up from Navy.

Navy: Where are you? Theo's asking, but I covered for you. Just let me know if you're okay.

Double shit. I'm beyond late for my shift at Ember. I drag myself up off the floor, splash ice-cold water on my face, and try to pull myself together. Like I can somehow wash away the fact that my entire life plan just went *poof*.

"You can do this," I tell my reflection, trying to sound convincing. "You're Clover fucking James. You've survived worse."

The woman in the mirror stares back at me with red-rimmed eyes that call me a liar.

Four hours into my shift at Ember, and I'm barely keeping it together.

The nausea hits me in waves, each one worse than the last. I've been choking back vomit every few minutes while mixing drinks and pretending everything's normal. I'm popping Altoids every couple of minutes because the mint is the only thing that keeps me from puking, but I've had a few near misses.

And the stupid tin is already down to less than a quarter left.

My smile feels like it's been painted on with cheap Halloween makeup. It's fake as hell and probably terrifying if you look too close. Like a clown.

Yep, that's me. A clown.

It's Friday night, so of course we're completely slammed. Every seat at the bar is taken, and the high-tops are packed with groups of women ordering those complicated Instagram-worthy cocktails that take forever to make. Navy and I move around each other while we work, but I can tell she's watching me.

Imagine what she'd say if I lose the battle (or my Altoids run out) and throw up in one of the trashcans back here behind the bar.

I take a deep breath in through my nose and slowly blow it out of my mouth and try to focus on anything other than the smell of alcohol and sickeningly sweet juice mixing in the most disgusting way imaginable. How did I never notice how horrible it smells back here?

"You seriously look like death," she whispers as we pass each other behind the bar. "And that's the fourth time you've disappeared to the bathroom."

"It's just something I ate," I lie, pouring tequila for a banana margarita that I'm one hundred percent sure is going to make me vomit. Who the fuck orders a *banana* margarita? I gag but try to hide it with a cough. My hands are shaking so bad I almost miss the glass. "Not a big deal."

It's the biggest *deal.*

I want to tell her so bad, but it wouldn't be fair to tell her before I tell Banks, right? Or maybe I should just confess, and she can help me work through what the hell I'm gonna do.

She narrows her eyes at me in that way that says she's not

buying what I'm selling, but thankfully we're too slammed for her to interrogate me the way she normally would.

I make it another forty-five minutes before the strongest wave of nausea yet hits me like a wrecking ball. There's no fighting this one.

"Be right back," I barely manage to choke out in Navy's direction before I'm literally sprinting for the employee bathroom, slamming the door so hard the hinges rattle. I don't even have time to lock it before I'm on my knees, violently emptying my stomach into the toilet.

I'm still heaving when the door creaks open behind me. Navy doesn't say a word, just crouches beside me and gathers my hair back from my sweaty face with one hand while the other rubs circles on my back. Tears burn my eyes when I remember Banks doing this exact same thing two weeks ago the first time this happened.

"Just something you ate, huh?" she says when I finally stop heaving. There's no judgment in her voice, just concern.

When I'm sure there's nothing left in my stomach to come up, I collapse back against the wall, completely drained. The cold tile feels amazing against my sweaty skin. I close my eyes because I can't look at her. Can't face what I know she's already figured out because Navy's always been too damn smart for her own good.

"So," she says quietly. "How far along are you?"

My eyes open but they're so damn heavy. I barely have it in me to pretend I don't know what she's talking about or that I don't want to curl up against my bestie and pour out the entire story. "What?"

"Clover." She sits down next to me on the grimy bathroom floor—without laying down a paper towel first, which tells me how worried she actually is. Her face is dead serious, not a trace of her usual snark. "I've known you for four years. I can tell the difference between food poisoning and *this*. Plus, you're running to the bathroom every five minutes and you literally dry heaved when Jim Kearney walked by with his cologne that you normally like." She raises an eyebrow. "I mix drinks for a living, but contrary to popular belief, that doesn't make me an idiot."

The tears I've been fighting all day finally break free. Once they start, it's like someone turned on a faucet I don't know how to shut off.

"Six weeks," I whisper, my voice breaking. Saying it out loud makes it real in a way that even those two pink lines didn't. "I found out this afternoon."

Navy doesn't look shocked. Not even a little bit. She just nods and takes my hand, squeezing it tight enough that I feel anchored to something solid when everything else is spinning out of control.

"Banks?" she asks.

I can't even get words out. Just nod and sob harder, which is super cute and professional in the employee bathroom of the bar I'm supposed to be running right now.

"Have you told him yet?"

"Are you kidding me?" The laugh that bursts out of me sounds borderline unhinged and it's snotty and gross, too. "I'm still trying to convince myself this isn't some horrible joke. How am I supposed to tell him? What am I supposed to say?"

"I don't know—maybe 'Banks, I'm pregnant with your baby'? Short, sweet, gets the point across." She's trying to make me laugh, but the reality of what I'm facing sobers me up real quick.

"He's going to think I trapped him," I whisper, finally giving voice to the fear that's been clawing at my insides since I saw those two lines. "This is Banks Priestly we're talking about. Mr. No-Strings-Attached. Mr. I-Don't-Do-Relationships. He definitely doesn't do *babies*." I wrap my arms around my stomach, this weird protective instinct I didn't know I had kicking in.

"And we both agreed that night was a mistake. A onetime thing that shouldn't have happened."

Navy rolls her eyes. "Yeah, because you two are just *so good* at being honest with yourselves and each other." She grabs my shoulders and makes me look her in the eye. "Listen to me, Clover James. That man looks at you like you personally hung the stars in the sky just so he'd have something pretty to look at. And you're no better. If he walks away from this—from you—then he's not who I think he is. And you?" She tightens her grip. "You're the strongest person I know. You've got this."

Her unwavering belief in me just makes me cry harder. "I don't know if I can do this," I sob out.

"You absolutely can." She squeezes my shoulders. "But here's the thing—you don't have to do it alone. Whatever happens with Banks, you've got me. And Kasen."

Oh god. *Kasen.* My stomach drops all over again.

How the hell am I going to tell my overprotective big brother that his best friend knocked me up? He's going to murder Banks and then lock me in a tower somewhere.

"Hey, one disaster at a time," Navy says, clearly reading the panic on my face. "First, talk to Banks. Then you two can figure out how to deal with your brother."

She helps me stand up on my wobbly legs and grabs a paper towel, wetting it in the sink before handing it to me. "I'm covering the rest of your shift. Go home, get some sleep, and figure out what you're going to say to Firefighter Hottie. And for the love of god brush your goddamn teeth."

I snort out a watery laugh. "I can't just bail on you—"

"Yes, you absolutely can. I already texted Chris to come in early, and Theo thinks you have food poisoning." She's basically shoving me toward the door. "Go. Home. Clover."

I don't have the energy to fight her on this. Or anything, really. I just nod and grab my purse from the office, then slip out the back door of Ember into the night.

The fifteen-minute walk home is pure torture. My thoughts chase themselves in circles, each one more panicked than the last. *What if he freaks out? What if he leaves? What if he wants to be involved but doesn't want me? What if he actually wants both of us?*

That last one scares me the most.

14
Clover

BY THE TIME I reach my apartment building, I've worked myself into such a state that I have to stop and take about twenty deep breaths before my hands stop shaking enough to get the key in the lock.

Banks isn't home. Thank god. Relief washes over me, followed immediately by a wave of guilt because I'm such a coward. I'm going to have to tell him—and soon—but right now I'm just pathetically grateful for a few hours to figure out what the hell I'm going to say.

I strip off my work clothes that reek of vomit and booze, take a shower, brush my teeth, then pull on my softest, most worn-in pajamas. The ones with the hole in the knee and the faded words across the chest. The ones Banks always smirks at when he sees me in them.

As if I don't have enough to deal with, now I'm thinking about his stupid smirk.

I need to bake. To work out what I'm going to do.

By the time I'm tired enough to sit down, I've got bread dough rising on the counter, a batch of chocolate chip cookies in the oven, and I'm elbow-deep in pie crust. My kitchen looks like a bakery exploded in it, and I keep having to wipe tears away with my forearm to avoid getting flour paste on my face. The apartment smells like vanilla and cinnamon and butter, but even the comfort of baking can't settle the tornado in my chest. I'm going to have to tell Banks that our onetime mistake is now an eighteen-year commitment.

I put the kettle on for ginger tea and sink into a chair at my kitchen table. I don't even clean up after myself, which normally would make me itch in my brain until I fixed it. I try to imagine how the conversation might go, playing it out in my head from every angle over and over and over again.

But no matter how I imagine it going, it always ends in disaster.

⛈

For the next three days, I watch Banks like I'm seeing him for the first time.

I notice things I've been pretending not to see for weeks. Like how he fixes stuff around the apartment without being asked or expecting praise. How he leaves my favorite blueberry muffin on the counter with a stupid note that says *Eat me, Freckles* ;). How he remembers I like extra cinnamon in my coffee and adds just the right amount every single time without me having to ask. The way his entire face transforms when he laughs at those ridiculous reality shows we've started watching together—his arm stretched across the back of the couch behind me, not quite touching but close enough that I can feel his body heat radiating toward me like a human furnace.

The terrifying truth slams into me during one of these quiet moments: I can see a future with him. A real one. Where we're more than temporary roommates or a one-night stand that resulted in an oops baby. Where this tiny person growing inside me has his laugh and my stubbornness and both of us to love them.

It scares the absolute shit out of me how badly I want that future. How possible it seems in these quiet moments when we're just existing together in a comfortable silence that makes this apartment feel more like home than it ever did before he moved in.

But nothing says "shit just got real" quite like a positive pregnancy test, and on the fourth day after discovering those two pink lines, reality comes crashing back when Kasen shows up at my door completely unannounced.

"There's my favorite sister!" he says, pulling me into a bear hug that lifts me off my feet.

My stomach immediately revolts. I swallow hard against the wave of nausea as he swings me around like I'm not growing a tiny human that really doesn't appreciate the motion. "I'm your only sister, dumbass."

He sets me down with a grin, then does that stupid complicated handshake-into-bro-hug thing with Banks that all guys seem programmed to do. It makes me roll my eyes so hard I'm surprised they don't fall out of my head.

"How's the roommate situation working out? Has she organized your socks by length and then color yet?" Kasen asks Banks, thinking he's hilarious.

"Every time I do laundry," Banks answers with that stupid smirk that makes my stomach do a series of gymnastics moves that have absolutely nothing to do with morning sickness (okay, constant all-day sickness). "But I've been secretly reorganizing her linen closet to get even."

"Which is a direct violation of house rule number eight," I point out, crossing my arms over my chest partly to look stern but mostly because I'm freaking out that Kasen's going to realize something's off, and I need the distance before the guilt eats me alive and I blurt out the truth before I've even told Banks.

Kasen looks between us, eyebrows climbing toward his hairline. "Huh. You two seem to be getting along way better than I expected."

There's something in his tone that makes my heart skip. Does he know something? Has Banks said something to him? Oh god, can he somehow tell I'm pregnant just by looking at me?

"So," I say quickly, desperate to change the subject, "What's up? Please don't tell me you're asking for another favor, because I'm still recovering from the last one." I try to make it sound like a joke, but there's a sharp edge to my voice that even I can hear, and Banks tilts his head, those hazel eyes I'm weak for sweeping over me like he knows something's off.

"Actually," Kasen says, dropping onto my couch like he owns the place, "I came to tell Banks the good news in person. His apartment is finally going to be ready next week." My brother turns toward his best friend who's taken the other side of the couch. "I ran into your landlord this morning while I was getting coffee, and he asked me to let you know."

The room goes completely silent. Like, hear-a-pin-drop silent. My whole body freezes as my eyes dart to Banks, who looks just as blindsided as I feel.

"That's..." Banks clears his throat, and I swear I see something like panic flash across his face. My own heart's staging an absolute riot against my ribs at the thought of him not being here anymore and for some stupid reason my eyes prickle. "That's great. Thanks for letting me know."

"Figured you'd be stoked to get out of this tiny place and back to your own space," Kasen continues, completely oblivious to the fact that he just dropped a nuclear bomb in my living room. "Plus, I'm sure Clover's dying to have her couch back, right sis?"

I force my face into what I hope resembles a normal human smile but probably looks more like I'm having a stroke. "Yeah. Totally."

The conversation keeps going around me, but I'm not even there anymore. It's like I'm floating above my body, watching myself nod at the right moments while my brain screams one thing on repeat:

Banks is leaving in a week. Banks is leaving in a week. Banks is leaving in a week.

And he has absolutely no idea he's about to become a father.

I have to tell him. Soon. Before I lose my nerve completely.

⛈️

I spend the entire next day rehearsing what to say. I practice in the bathroom mirror while brushing my teeth, with Mai Tai, the Pothos that lives on my bedroom floor, in the shower where no one can see me cry, during my Business Ethics class where I should be paying attention but instead, I'm writing and rewriting this impossible speech in my head.

Nothing sounds right. Nothing feels big enough for news that's literally going to change his life forever.

By the time Banks's shift ends, I'm a complete nervous wreck. I've paced so many circles in my living room I'm surprised the downstairs neighbors haven't banged on their ceiling. I've stress-baked enough cookies to feed half the city. I've thrown up at least four times, and I've changed my outfit so many times I lost count before saying screw it and putting on the same damn leggings and oversized sweater I started with.

The sound of his key in the lock makes my heart climb into my throat, and for a second I think I might throw up again.

The door swings open, and there he is—all six-foot-two of

firefighter perfection, still in the joggers he wears to the gym that show off *everything* and a navy blue PFD t-shirt that stretches across those ridiculous shoulders of his. The same shoulders I dug my nails into six weeks ago, which is exactly how we ended up in this mess.

His usual easy smile dies the second he sees me. "What happened? Are you okay?"

The immediate concern in his voice is enough for my stupid *hormones* to go into overdrive and make me want to both melt into a puddle at his feet and cry while he feeds me cookies and kisses me until I can't breathe.

This is exactly what Navy was talking about—the way he's always looking out for me, always ready to jump in front of a metaphorical (and probably literal) bullet if I need him to. Even when I insist I don't need anyone. Even when I've pushed him away every chance I get because I'm terrified of how he makes me feel.

"I'm okay," I say, but my voice comes out all wobbly and pathetic. "But we need to talk."

He sets his gym bag down slowly, his eyes locked on my face like he's trying to figure out what's wrong before I even say it. "Okay."

"Maybe you should sit down for this."

He doesn't budge an inch. "I'm fine right here."

Of course he is. The man has never once in his life done what I've asked him to.

I take a deep breath that's supposed to be calming but doesn't help at all. Every word I came up with, every speech I've practiced all day has completely vanished from my brain. All that's left is the terrifying truth I need to spit out before I lose my nerve completely.

"I'm pregnant," I blurt out while he's bent over unlacing his boots, my fingers clasped together so hard my knuckles are white. "It's yours. Obviously."

Banks freezes with one boot half-unlaced like someone hit pause on him. For what feels like the longest moment of my entire life, he doesn't move, doesn't speak, doesn't even seem to breathe. Then, slowly, he straightens up, and his face is completely unreadable.

"You're pregnant," he repeats, his voice flat.

I nod, not trusting my voice to work.

"You're sure?" His eyes dart down to my stomach, then back up to my face.

"I haven't gone to the doctor or anything, but I don't think three tests, a missed period, and constant throwing up for the last two weeks are wrong." I wrap my arms around myself because I suddenly feel freezing cold despite the fact that it's like eighty degrees in my apartment. "From the night of the storm." *Way to state the obvious, Clover. It's not like you've been sleeping with anyone else. Or Banks again.* "We didn't... You didn't wear a condom and I'm not on birth control."

The silence stretches so long I swear I can hear the seconds ticking by on the clock in the kitchen. His continued silence feels like a rejection, like he's mentally mapping the fastest route to the door and out of my life forever. I can literally feel my walls going back up, protecting me from what I know is coming next.

"You don't have to be involved," I say, the words rushing out so fast they trip over each other. "I know this isn't what you signed up for when you moved in. I just... I thought you deserved to know before you leave next week. I'm not asking for anything."

Something flashes across his face—shock? Anger? Hurt? I genuinely can't tell, and it makes my stomach twist into another knot. It's a whole damn pretzel factory in there right now.

"Is that what you really think of me?" His voice is so quiet I have to strain to hear him. "That I'd just walk away from this?

From you? From our baby?" He takes a step closer with every question until he's standing in front of me, and I have to tilt my chin up to look at him.

The way he says "our baby" makes something in my chest break wide open.

Before I can respond, Banks moves with a suddenness that steals my breath. His hands slam against the wall on either side of my head, caging me in. The impact makes me jump, but there's no fear—only a rush of heat that floods my body when he leans in close enough that I can feel his breath on my face.

What is it with us and walls?

Now's not the time, Clover.

"Let me make something perfectly fucking clear," he growls, his voice dropping to that dangerous register that turns my insides to liquid. "I don't walk away. Not from responsibilities, not from people I care about, and sure as hell not from the woman carrying my child."

His eyes burn into mine, fierce and unblinking. I'm trapped between the solid wall at my back and the wall of muscle that is Banks Priestly in front of me. I should feel cornered, threatened even. Instead, my treacherous body is practically humming with awareness, my nipples tightening painfully against my shirt as his scent—fresh air and smoke and pure Banks—overwhelms me.

"You think I don't want to be here?" he continues, his face so close to mine our noses almost touch. "I can't sleep unless I know you're safe. I don't hold your hair back when you're sick or help you study or watch those stupid fucking shows with you because I have to. For someone so smart, you can be incredibly fucking dense, Clover."

He's so close I can see the gold flecks in his hazel eyes. My heart hammers against my ribs so hard I wonder if he can hear it.

"Banks—" I whisper, but he cuts me off.

"No." He shakes his head, one hand moving to cup my cheek with a gentleness that's completely different from the fierce expression on his face. "I'm not done. I'm here because the thought of being anywhere else—of not being the one who takes care of you, who makes sure you eat, who feels our baby kick for the first time—would fucking destroy me. Do you understand?"

I can only nod, my voice caught somewhere in my throat as his thumb traces over my cheekbone.

"Good," he says, and then he's pushing away from the wall, leaving me breathless and unsteady.

Then he does the absolute last thing I'm expecting.

He drops to his knees in front of me.

His hands—those big, capable hands that have pulled people from burning buildings and fixed my leaky shower and cooked me dinner—come to rest on my hips. Then, like I'm made of glass, one hand slides to my stomach. His touch is so gentle, so reverent, that tears immediately flood my eyes.

"Clover James," he says, and his voice breaks on my name as tears fall in rivers down my face. There's no stopping them. It's a full-on flood. "There hasn't been a damn thing casual about you and me, not since the moment I met you."

Whatever walls I've been desperately trying to rebuild around my heart just completely crumble at his words. I couldn't stop the tears now if my life depended on it.

"I'm not going anywhere," he says, and then—oh my god— he presses his forehead against my stomach, like somehow he's already talking to our baby. Our *baby*. "You hear me? This isn't just about the baby, Clover. It's about you. It's always been about you."

His words unlock something in my chest that's been rusted shut for so long I forgot it was even there. This hope I've never let myself feel, this future I've been too terrified to imagine because I was so sure it could never be real.

"Banks," I whisper, reaching out to touch his hair before I can stop myself. It's soft between my fingers, still a little damp from his post-shift shower, and he leans into my touch like a man dying of thirst who just found water.

"I know," he says, his lips moving against my shirt, against my stomach where our baby is growing. The words are a little muffled but there's no mistaking them. "I'm not going back to my apartment next week, and you better not try to make me."

A sob rips its way out of my chest, and suddenly his arms are around me, holding me up as my knees completely give out. We end up on the floor together, his big body curled around mine like he's trying to protect me from the world, while I cry all over his chest.

"I'm scared," I admit between hiccupping sobs. "I'm so fucking scared, Banks."

"I know," he says, his lips pressed against my hair. "Me too. But we're gonna figure this out. You and me."

"You and me," I repeat, and the words feel strange in my mouth. But they also feel right.

His hand finds its way back to my stomach, and I cover it with mine without even thinking, linking our fingers together. For the first time since I saw those two pink lines, the panic that's been choking me starts to loosen its grip. In its place is something that feels dangerously like hope.

"I'm not going anywhere," he whispers into my hair. "Not a chance in hell. You can't make me."

And despite all my fears, despite the walls I've spent years building to keep everyone out, despite the fact that my life plan has been my safety blanket for as long as I can remember—I actually believe him.

15
Banks

IT'S BEEN two weeks since Clover told me I'm going to be a father, and I still can't wrap my head around it.

I wake up every morning in her bed—though it's basically our bed now—and for about three seconds, everything feels normal. Then it hits me all over again: I'm going to be a dad. There's a tiny human growing inside the woman sleeping basically on top of me. A human we made together, one that's half her and half me and it's a straight up mindfuck.

A human that's turned me into a complete paranoid lunatic who's one internet search away from bubble-wrapping the entire apartment.

In fact, I've never seen her look more beautiful than she does right now—warm, sleepy, and carrying our baby.

My morning wood twitches against the thigh she's got draped over my hips, but neither of us acknowledges it.

"Can't help it," I say, running a fingertip over the curve of her cheek, counting the scatter of freckles that've driven me crazy for years. The ones I've now memorized. "You sprouted more of these overnight. There're at least three new ones."

One eye cracks open. "Not possible."

"It's totally possible. Pregnancy does weird shit, Freckles. I read about it in one of the books."

She groans, dragging a pillow over her face. "If you quote another pregnancy book at me, I swear to God, I'll scream. I thought I was the one with the organizational kink in this relationship."

This relationship. Those words light me the fuck up inside. It's like Christmas up in here right down to my bones. We haven't exactly defined what we are to each other—we're too busy adjusting to the nuclear bomb that is "surprise, we're having a baby"—but I'm calling it a win that she's stopped insisting we made a mistake. That she's letting me stay in her bed every night, even if she still pretends I'm technically living on her couch.

That's Clover for you—stubborn as all hell.

"Speaking of kinks," I murmur, sliding my hand beneath the blankets, settling it on the warm skin of her hip. "Have I mentioned how unbelievably sexy you are in the morning?"

Both eyes pop open. "We have an ultrasound in an hour."

"Plenty of time." I counter, flipping our positions so she's lying flat on the bed and ducking under the covers to press my lips to her stomach. "Morning, Peanut," I whisper against her skin before trailing kisses lower.

Clover's laugh turns into a gasp when I reach my destination. Her fingers tangle in my hair, tugging enough to make my cock throb as I nudge her panties to the side. "You're impossible."

"Mmm, that's not what you said last night when you were screaming my name."

"Banks." There's a warning in her voice, but it's undermined by the way her thighs fall open to give me better access.

"Clover." I match her tone, arching a filthy smirk up the length of her body. "Let me make you feel good."

She's putty in my hands after that—not that I'm keeping

score—and by the time I've made her come twice, once with my mouth and once with my cock buried so deep inside her that I swear I feel my soul connect with hers, we're cutting it dangerously close to being late.

"This is your fault," she accuses as we tear around the apartment looking for her other shoe. "I told you we didn't have time."

"Worth it." I snag her by the waist as she rushes past, stealing a quick kiss. "The way you look when you come around my cock is my new favorite show. I'd watch it on repeat."

Her face flushes that delicious shade of pink that makes me want to take her back to bed and start all over again. "You can't just say stuff like that."

"Why not? It's true."

"Because—" She stops, sighs. "Because it makes me want to climb you like a tree instead of going to this appointment."

Navy called it. "I'm one hundred percent on board with that plan."

"Banks." She swats my chest, but there's no heat in it. "This is serious. We're actually going to see our baby today."

The reality of her words sobers me right the hell up. *Our baby.* We're going to see it—*him? her?*—on a screen. Hear the heartbeat. Make it real in a way that nothing else has.

"Yeah," I say, suddenly just as serious as she is. "We are."

The look we exchange is loaded with everything we haven't said to each other yet. All the fear, the excitement, the absolute terror of stepping into this new chapter together. In that moment, I have a flash of clarity so strong it steals my breath: I want everything with this woman. The whole package. The picket fence, the rings, the happily ever after. Not just because she's carrying my child, but because she's the only person who's ever made me feel like I'm home just by existing.

But telling her that right now would send her running. If

there's one thing I've learned about Clover James in the past six months, it's that she's as skittish as a wild animal when it comes to anything that threatens her independence.

So instead, I fish her missing shoe out from under the coffee table, present it with an exaggerated flourish like some knock-off Prince Charming, and say, "Come on, Freckles—let's go see our kid."

The waiting room at Dr. Reed Walker's office is teeming with pregnant women, and I'm trying and failing not to stare. Not gonna lie, it's freaking me out a little, coming face to face with my future.

There's one that's gotta be at least six months along—belly sticking out like she swallowed a basketball. Another looks on the verge of popping any second—she can't sit still for shit, probably because she's so uncomfortable. Then there's someone who doesn't even look pregnant, like Clover, but her hand cradles her stomach in that instinctive, protective gesture that's a dead giveaway.

Sure, I've seen plenty of pregnant women on calls—shit, I even delivered a baby once—but this is the first time I'm surrounded by them since learning I'll be a dad.

Will this be us in a few months? It has to be, right? The alternative is unthinkable, and I break out in a cold sweat even at the brief thought something might happen to my baby. And how the hell is Clover's tiny body going to stretch out like that? She's already changing—her tits fuller in my hands, nipples so sensitive she gasps when I barely touch them. The nausea hits her hardest right when her shift at Ember should be starting but it's there all the time. And she crashes at the most random times, just shuts down and passes out with zero energy left for anything but growing the tiny life inside her.

And it's my job to protect them both, to do everything in my power to make sure they're safe.

My knee's going a thousand miles a minute, bouncing up and down while I pretend to read some parenting magazine I can't focus on. Meanwhile, Clover's the picture of calm beside me, scrolling through her phone and scribbling notes in that color-coded planner she carries everywhere and treats like the Holy Grail.

"You're making the whole bench shake," she says without looking up. "What's got you so worked up?"

"Nothing." Yeah, that's a total lie. I'm freaking the fuck out but I'm not about to admit it. Not when I'm supposed to be here so she can lean on me. I'm trying to show her that I'm always going to show up and she can count on me. Losing my shit at the OBGYN's office isn't going to earn me any points toward winning her over and convincing her she needs me in her life.

"Banks." Finally, she tears her eyes from her phone and hits me with that look—one eyebrow arched, seeing right through my bullshit. "Your leg's bouncing so hard I'm getting motion sickness."

I try to force my knee to stay still, but all that nervous energy just reroutes to my fingers, which start drumming against my thigh.

"I'm just thinking."

"About?" She's not letting this go. I shouldn't have expected anything less.

"Whether I'll be a good dad." The words just fall out before I can stop them. I haven't told her about the nightmares screwing with my sleep. The ones where I'm working a forty-eight-hour shift and miss the birth completely. Where I'm just like my old man—physically present but mentally checked out, more committed to the job than to my family. Where Clover and the baby need me and I'm too busy pulling strangers from burning buildings to be there for them.

Her face goes all soft and sweet and she grabs my hand, lacing our fingers together. Her touch kills the storm in my head and I blow out a breath.

"You're going to be an amazing dad, Banks."

"How do you know?"

"Because I've seen how you are with people you care about." She squeezes my hand and I squeeze hers right back. "I've watched you for years, how protective you get. How you always show up, even when it's hard. Especially when it's hard."

The rush her words give me is like the high I get after we successfully rescue someone from a burning building but more. Bigger, Stronger.

"Yeah?" I can't keep the stupid grin off my face. My chest feels like it's about to burst wide open. Hell, I need to hear her say it again.

She rolls her eyes, but her gaze is dead serious. "Yes, dumbass. Our baby is lucky to have you." Then her voice dips to this quiet whisper, and I have to lean in to hear her. "I'm lucky to have you, too."

Holy shit. Did Clover James just admit she has feelings for me? After years of pretending she barely tolerates my existence? I want to yank her into my arms, kiss her until she's breathless, maybe never let go. But before I can even wrap my head around what she said, a nurse steps into the waiting room and calls Clover's name.

And just like that, we're being lead into an exam room.

16
Banks

IT ALL HAPPENS FAST after that. Clover disappears behind a curtain to change into one of those paper gowns that leave your ass hanging out, and I try not to pace the five square feet of available space while I wait. A nurse bustles in to take her vitals and fires off a million questions that Clover answers with that calm way she has when she's in manager mode. I love watching her like this—so capable and in control.

It gets me hard as fuck. Or it would, if I wasn't currently losing my shit.

Then we're alone again and I run my hand through my hair and start pacing again. No way can I sit still right now.

"It's going to be okay," she says, reaching for my hand from where she's sitting on the exam table in that crinkling paper dress thing. "We've got this."

We. I swear that one word just kicked me in the fucking chest. Not her and me separately, but us. A team. After everything, after all the times she's shoved me away, now she's telling me we're in this together. There's no chance in hell I'm taking that for granted.

The door swings open, and in walks Dr. Reed Walker. Yeah,

the same Dr. Walker I pretty much cyberstalked last week. The one I made a fucking PowerPoint presentation about to convince Clover he was the best OBGYN in Portland. The one with the perfect track record, zero malpractice suits, and a waiting list a mile long that I somehow got us on by calling in a favor from a battalion chief whose wife works in hospital administration.

But shit, no one bothered to mention in all those five-star reviews that he'd be this young and good-looking. He's tall with perfect hair and a jawline better than mine. And suddenly I'm regretting all those hours I spent convincing Clover this was the guy who should have his hands all over her.

"You must be Clover and Banks," he says with a professional smile, extending his hand first to her. "I'm Dr. Walker. Pleasure to meet you both."

I move to stand beside Clover, my fingers wrapping around the back of her neck as I shake his hand with my other one. Maybe I squeeze a little harder than necessary. Do I feel like an asshole? Yup. Do I care? Nope.

"Nice to meet you," I manage through clenched teeth.

Clover shoots me a look that clearly says *what the actual fuck are you doing?* but I catch the little twitch at the corner of her mouth and the tension in my shoulders loosens. I think she likes me being a possessive dick, at least a little.

"I've heard great things from Janet in administration," Dr. Walker goes on, still smiling like I didn't just attempt to crush his fingers. "She mentioned you're with Portland Fire. Battalion Chief Ramirez speaks very highly of you."

"Yeah, Ramirez is a good guy," I say, not even pretending to be interested in chit-chat. I want to see my kid on that ultrasound. "I owe him one for pulling some strings to get us in here so fast."

Dr. Walker nods, parks himself on a rolling stool, and starts tapping away on a tablet that I assume holds Clover's chart. He gets right down to business, which I appreciate despite my irrational dislike of him.

"Based on your last period and everything you've told me, you're about eight weeks along," he says, looking up at Clover. "How have you been feeling so far?"

"Like absolute garbage," she admits, and I hate how pale she looks under these fluorescent lights. "The nausea is basically constant but gets way worse at night. Try making fancy cocktails when the smell of alcohol makes you want to puke your guts out."

He nods like he's heard this a million times. "That's very typical. I can prescribe something if it's interfering with your work." He makes a note on the tablet. "Any other symptoms? Fatigue? Breast tenderness?"

"Both," she says, and her cheeks turn this adorable shade of pink. "Lots of both."

I can vouch for the breast tenderness. I barely brushed against her nipple this morning and she nearly jumped out of her skin. But I'm keeping my mouth shut since Clover's doing a great job of speaking for herself.

"All completely normal." Dr. Walker gives her one of those reassuring doctor smiles. "Now, how about we take a look at your baby?"

Your baby? It's *our* baby, Doc.

But I bite my tongue, because all I really care about is seeing that tiny heartbeat flicker on the screen. And maybe making sure Dr. Perfect Hair doesn't get too handsy with the mother of my child.

Dr. Walker starts prepping for the ultrasound, and I'm bracing myself for the classic scene you see in movies—gel on her belly, that little wand moving around. But no, apparently at eight weeks, it's some hardcore next-level shit, because he pulls out a wand that looks straight out of porn, complete with a condom on top.

"At this stage," he explains like I'm not about to be booked for murder, "we'll need a transvaginal ultrasound. The baby's still too small to see clearly using the abdominal method."

"Sorry, a what now?" I blurt out before I can rein in my jealous bullshit. My heart is pumping so hard I can hear it in my ears at the thought of what's about to happen. My desire to see my baby and my instinct to get Dr. Walker the fuck away from Clover are at war inside of me and I don't know which side is going to win. I've gotta admit—I didn't see this coming. "You're gonna put that thing where?"

Clover nearly crushes my fingers in her grip. "Banks," she hisses. "Shut. Up. This is normal."

Dr. Walker has the decency to pretend not to hear me. "It won't hurt, just some mild discomfort. I'll be quick and gentle."

I chew the inside of my cheek hard enough to taste blood while he readies that fucking dildo wand. Why the fuck didn't any of those books mention this? Or maybe they did, and I blocked it out. Either way, seeing some other dude slip anything inside Clover has me seeing red. But I force it down—this is about our baby, not my issues.

I picked Dr. Walker for a reason, and I need to deal.

Clover clutches my hand tighter as he dims the lights. I've seen horrible shit on the job—charred remains, telling parents their kid didn't make it—but right now, watching another man get all up in my woman's business might be where I finally snap.

And then I hear it: a furious *whoosh-whoosh-whoosh*, so loud it blows everything else out of my head, jealousy included.

"There's your baby's heartbeat," Dr. Walker says, shifting the wand. "Nice and strong, exactly what we want."

Time fucking stops. My brain can't process what's happening. That sound—that impossibly fast rhythm that's going a million miles an hour—is coming from inside Clover. That's my kid's heart. Our baby is real and alive and has a heartbeat.

I stare at the monitor, where a tiny blob—kind of kidney-bean-shaped—sits in the middle. It's so small I can barely believe it's a person. But there's a flicker in the center, like a little firefly blinking on and off, and my own heart feels like it's about to explode.

"Holy shit," I choke, my voice cracking. I'm squeezing Clover's hand so hard she flinches, but I can't bring myself to let go. "That's—that's really our baby? That little thing?"

Dr. Walker nods, his face softening and okay, he's a decent dude when I don't want to break every one of his fingers. "That's your baby. See this flickering?" He points to the screen. "That's the heart. Everything looks exactly as it should at eight weeks."

My vision goes blurry, and it takes me a second to realize I'm fucking crying. In front of Clover. In front of Dr. Walker. Tears running down my face as I stare at this tiny blob that's half me, half her. I'm crying over this tiny accidental peanut that's suddenly the most important thing in my universe.

I glance at Clover and see she's already looking up at me, tears in her own eyes. "Banks," she breathes, and the sound of her saying my name right now—like a prayer—almost undoes me. She's feeling the same insane wonder, the same *holy shit, this is happening* that I am.

I press my forehead to hers, not giving a single fuck that we have an audience. "I know," I whisper. And I do. I fucking feel it all.

Dr. Walker gives us a minute while he takes measurements, typing notes into his tablet. I finally manage to get my shit together and look back at the screen where he's frozen the image of our baby.

"Everything looks perfect," he says, like it's no big deal. But perfect is my new favorite word. "Perfect size, perfect heartbeat. You've got a healthy little one in there."

Relief slams into me, nearly knocking me on my ass. "So

there's nothing wrong? No problems? Baby's good?" I sound desperate because I am.

Dr. Walker's face shifts into serious-doctor mode. "All pregnancies have risks, especially first pregnancies. But given Clover's age and health, she's at lower risk. We'll just keep monitoring."

My brain latches onto that word—*risk*—and won't let go. Like a fucking pit bull with a steak. "What kind of risks exactly? Preeclampsia? Gestational diabetes? Placenta previa? Preterm labor? HELLP syndrome?"

Clover and Dr. Walker stare at me like I've sprouted another head.

"Have you been reading medical textbooks?" Dr. Walker asks, his eyebrows raised.

I shrug, feeling a bit dumb for exposing my late-night Wikipedia and Google binges. "I, uh, wanted to be prepared. I may have gotten a little carried away with the research."

Clover eyes me. "A *little*?"

"Okay, so I might have ordered every pregnancy book Amazon sells, joined some online dad forums, subscribed to a few medical journals..." I rake a hand through my hair, pulling the ends the way I always do when I've got anxious energy to burn. "I just wanted to know what we might be facing."

Dr. Walker actually looks impressed. "That level of involvement is great. But there's no sign Clover's at increased risk for any complications. She's healthy, everything is *perfect* so far."

That word again. Perfect. My chest settles for the first time in weeks.

While Dr. Walker starts talking next steps, setting up appointments, I half-zone out. My hand's on Clover's belly, where our baby—*our actual fucking baby*—is growing at this exact moment.

Holy shit, we're really having a baby.

At some point, I've gotta tell Kasen I knocked up his sister.

My best friend's going to kill me, and I honestly can't blame him. If some dude knocked up my sister? I'd be plotting the most painful way to end them right about now.

But for once, none of that matters. Because we just heard our baby's heartbeat. And it's the most amazing thing I've ever heard in my life.

"—and I've sent the prescription for prenatal vitamins to your pharmacy," Dr. Walker is saying as I tune back in. "Do either of you have any questions?"

I bark out a laugh. "Uh, yeah—about a million. But I'll try to narrow it down so I don't waste your entire day."

He chuckles, and for the first time, he seems more like a normal dude than just a doctor. "In that case, here's my card." He offers it to me with a friendly nod. "It has my cell number. Most dads have random questions between appointments, so shoot me a text if anything comes up."

I glance down at the card, caught off guard. "That's—wow. Thanks, man. Appreciate it."

He just smiles like it's no big deal. "It's what I'm here for." Then he hands Clover a folder stuffed with papers. "Here are your ultrasound prints and some first-trimester info."

As we leave the office, I can't stop staring at the grainy black-and-white picture of our little peanut. I've pulled people from the worst car accidents imaginable. I've restarted hearts with my bare hands. But nothing—absolutely fucking nothing —has ever felt like this. Like seeing my kid's heart beating for the first time.

And somewhere between all that wonder, it slams into me that I have to tell Kasen about this before he hears it from somebody else. My best friend is going to lose his mind.

Clover's voice snaps me back as we walk to my truck. "You okay there? You haven't said a single word since we left the office."

I peel my gaze off the ultrasound to find her studying me

with this mix of concern and amusement. "Yeah, sorry. I'm just..." I hold up the photo, shaking my head in disbelief. "It's real, you know? There's a tiny person in there. Our tiny person."

"Trust me, puking my guts out all day already made it pretty real for me," she says, but she's smiling a little. When I wrap my arm around her waist, she actually leans into me instead of pulling away. That's new.

Definitely not complaining.

I press a quick kiss to her hair, breathing in the citrus scent of her shampoo. "I, uh, have something I want to show you when we get home."

She cranes her neck to look up at me. "Should I be nervous?"

I smirk, unable to help it. "Absolutely."

"What... is this?"

Clover's staring at the three-inch-thick binder I've just handed her like it might bite. The cover reads "Baby Priestly" in bold black letters.

"Research," I say, trying not to look as nervous as I feel while she flips it open and sees the color-coded tabs. "I wanted to be prepared."

"You made a binder." It's not a question. She looks from the organized pages to my face and back again like she can't decide if I'm joking. "A color-coded binder with..." She squints at the page, "is that a table of contents?"

"And an index," I add, which is definitely not helping based on how high her eyebrows just shot up. "Look, I know it seems like I went overboard—"

"You think?" She flips through more pages, eyes getting wider.

"—but I wanted to make sure we had all the information we'd need." I reach over and flip to the green section, our shoulders touching. "This part's all nutrition—what you should eat, what to avoid, supplements for brain development. Blue is exercise during pregnancy—what's safe, what'll hurt the baby. Yellow's broken down by trimester so we know what to expect. Red is all the warning signs, when to call Dr. Walker. Purple is different birthing options—"

"Birthing options," she echoes, running her finger along the edge of the page as I flip through. I can't tell if she's impressed or horrified. "You researched birthing options."

"Well, yeah." I rub the back of my neck, suddenly feeling like I've overstepped in a big way. "I know it's your body and ultimately your choice, but I thought we should at least know all the options."

A strange expression crosses her face. Not anger or annoyance like I expected, but something softer. Almost... touched? "I can't believe you did all this."

"Too much?" I ask, suddenly uncertain. Clover's the one who color-codes and organizes everything from her to-do lists to her damn underwear drawer. If anyone should appreciate this level of organization, it's her. But maybe I've crossed a line.

"No, it's..." She traces a chart showing fetal development by week. "It's actually amazing, Banks. I just—I didn't expect it."

Relief floods through me. I wanted to do this for her and do it in a way I knew she'd appreciate. That would meet her where she is. That would make her see that I get her. That her little quirks are the things I like best about her and if she needs me to color code and put things in order, I'll do it to make her happy. "I want to do this right, Freckles. All of it."

Her eyes lift to mine, that wall she usually keeps up between us nowhere to be seen. "You're really in this, aren't you? One hundred percent."

"One thousand percent," I correct, taking the binder and

setting it aside so I can tug her closer. "This isn't some obligation for me. I want this. I want our baby. I want—" *you*, I almost say, but manage to swallow it back at the last second. Too much, too soon. "I want us to do this together."

She nods, that new softness still shimmering in her eyes, and leans up to press a gentle kiss to my lips. "Thank you," she whispers, her breath warm against my mouth. "For the binder. For being here. For... everything."

It feels like the most important moment we've had since she told me she was pregnant. Like we're finally on the same page, building something together instead of dancing around each other.

Naturally, that's when I go and screw it up.

17
Banks

"FOR FUCK'S SAKE, Banks, I can carry a case of water on my own!" Clover's face is flushed as she yanks the plastic-wrapped package from my hands. "I'm pregnant, not helpless!"

It's been three days since the ultrasound, and apparently I've hit my limit of 'overprotective boyfriend' behavior. Not that we've slapped any official label on what we are. But I'm the one sleeping next to her at night, holding her hair back when morning sickness hits, driving her to doctors' appointments, cooking her dinner so she remembers to eat, and researching crib safety standards while she dozes on my chest.

So yeah, 'boyfriend' feels pretty accurate.

"You know the doctor said not to lift anything heavy," I argue, reaching for the water again. "And that's at least twenty pounds."

"Which is well within the guidelines you put in your own damn binder!" She sidesteps me, hauling the case onto the kitchen counter with a thud that makes me wince. "This is getting ridiculous. You're smothering me."

"I'm looking out for you. There's a difference."

"Is there? Because it feels a lot like you don't think I'm

capable of taking care of myself." Her hands go to her hips in that stance I've come to recognize as Clover digging in for a fight. "You've been on my ass every five minutes since the ultrasound. *Don't lift that. Don't eat that. Don't work so late. Drink more water. Take your vitamins.*"

My gut twists at how she's throwing my words back in my face, but hell if I can back down. "Those things matter," I say, keeping my tone as even as I can. "And you're working too damn hard. Theo would understand if you cut back. Standing on your feet all night can't be good for the baby."

Her eyes flash. "The baby is the size of a raspberry, Banks. Standing behind a bar for a few hours isn't going to hurt it." She flings her arms up in frustration. "And who's paying the bills if I cut my hours, huh? My rent won't pay itself. My bar fund sure as hell isn't going to magically appear."

I open my mouth, then snap it shut before I say what I'm actually thinking—that I'd happily support her, that I want her to move in with me permanently, that I've been scoping out houses in our price range because the apartment I've been paying for but not living in for months is too small for the three of us, and her place isn't much bigger. That I'm in love with her and want to give her everything.

Instead, what comes out is:

"Someone has to think about our kid's safety," I snap—and immediately realize I've fucked up. Clover's eyes go wide, then narrow to lethal slits.

"Is that what you think?" she demands, voice trembling at the edges. "That I can't be trusted to take care of myself or our child?"

"That's not what I meant—"

"Then what did you mean?" Her voice breaks, and my heart freefalls when I see tears in her eyes. Clover James, who never cries, not even when she cracked two ribs slipping on ice last winter. "Because it sure as hell sounds like you don't trust me."

"Clover—"

"No." She holds up a hand to cut me off, but I'm more focused on the other one, which has curled protectively over her stomach in a way that makes my throat tight. "I need a minute."

She slips past me and heads toward her bedroom—*our* bedroom, as I've come to think of it, even though it doesn't feel like that right now.

I give her five minutes, barely, before I follow. I can't stand the distance between us, especially not when she's pissed at me. The bedroom door is cracked open—a good sign, since she would have shut it if she really wanted to be alone.

She's sitting cross-legged on the bed, staring at the sonogram picture she's kept on her nightstand since the appointment. Her eyes are red, but her cheeks are dry. Even when she's upset, Clover hates letting anyone see her cry.

"I don't think you're irresponsible," I say quietly from the doorway. "And I do trust you with our baby."

She doesn't look up. "Then why are you treating me like I can't handle basic self-care? Like you've got to watch my every move?"

I step into the room, not sure how close I should get. "Because I'm terrified," I admit, the words torn from somewhere deep in my chest. "I'm so fucking scared, Clover."

That gets her attention. Her eyes snap to mine, confusion clear on her face. "Of what? You heard the doctor. Everything looks perfect."

"I'm scared of failing." I run a hand through my hair, pacing the small space of her bedroom. "Of not being there when you need me. Of something happening to you or the baby when I'm not around to protect you."

"Banks—"

"I spent my entire childhood wondering if my dad was going to come home," I continue, the words pouring out now that the dam has broken. "Every shift, every call, wondering if this was the time he wouldn't make it back. And even when he was around, he wasn't really there—he was either working, sleeping off a shift, or about to leave again. I barely knew him, Freckles." My voice breaks on her nickname. "I don't want our kid feeling like that about me."

She stands and comes toward me with a gentleness I don't deserve after how I've been acting. "That's not going to happen."

"You don't know that. My job—"

"Is dangerous, yes," she says, sliding her hands over mine and tangling our fingers. "But you're not your father, Banks. And I'm not telling you not to hover or worry—I'm just asking you to trust me a little. To let me breathe."

The fight drains out of me all at once. "I'm hovering like a total psycho, aren't I? The baby's not even born and I'm already a helicopter parent."

A small smile tugs at her lips. "At least you recognize it. That's the first step."

I tug her closer until my forehead rests against hers. "I just want to take care of you both," I murmur.

"I know." She pulls back enough to catch my gaze. "But you need to understand something. After my mom died, I spent years proving I could stand on my own two feet. That I didn't need anyone. It made me stubborn—and maybe too independent sometimes—but it's who I am."

I exhale slowly, raking my hand through my hair. "So you want me to back off."

"I'm telling you I need room to breathe," she corrects. "That's different."

I can't help a faint smirk. "You realize it's physically painful for me to watch you struggle and not jump in to help, right?"

She squeezes my hand. "Just like it's painful for me to accept help when I've spent so long proving I don't need it."

I stare at her for a long beat. She's so damn gorgeous—stubborn and brilliant and unstoppable. "You're actual sunshine, you know that?" I say. "Stubborn as hell, but the brightest thing in my life."

She laughs under her breath. "And you're a storm cloud, always hovering and threatening to rain all over my independence parade."

I slide my arms around her waist. "Someone's gotta carry an umbrella when you insist on dancing in the downpour," I say, pulling her in until her head's tucked under my chin and she's snug against my chest. "You're gonna give me a heart attack one day, Freckles."

"And you're gonna suffocate me under your giant, overprotective man-blanket of worry."

I snort a laugh. "Man-blanket of worry?"

"Hey, give me shit all you want, but my creative brain power is currently being stolen by this." She points at her stomach, but her lips are curving in a real smile now.

I cup her face, feeling the tension between us easing finally easing up. "All right, here's the deal: I'll try to tone down the overprotectiveness if you promise to ask for help before you're about to collapse from exhaustion, okay?"

"Your proposal is acceptable," she says, making her voice deeper to imitate the alien from *Men in Black,* and then she cracks herself up. God, she's fucking cute.

Eventually, she sobers, running her fingers along my stubble. "We're both afraid of ghosts, aren't we?"

"Yeah." I swallow, nodding. "I'm scared of not becoming my father, and you're scared of needing anyone. We make quite a pair, Freckles."

She snuggles closer, tucking her head back under my chin. "We do, but we'll figure it out."

I hold her tight, because I can't stand having space between us. "Yeah," I say quietly. "We will."

"And I'll work on letting you help," she promises, sliding

her arms around my waist. "We've gotta find a balance or we're going to drive each other insane."

"Too late, Freckles." I brush a strand of hair off her cheek. "I lost my mind over you a long time ago."

She flushes at that, the kind of blush that makes my blood run hot. Not as good as the flush she gets with my cock inside her, but damn close.

"Let's make a deal," she says, plowing straight past the compliment like she always does. "You ease up on the whole caveman thing, and I'll start including you in decisions. Let you know when I need help."

"Deal," I agree immediately—knowing full well this is the best outcome I'm getting with my stubborn woman. "But can I make one request?"

Her eyes narrow, already suspicious. "What?"

"Let me show you something." I pull my phone from my pocket, nerves kicking in despite myself. "I've been doing some research."

She raises an eyebrow. "More? On what?"

"Pregnancy-safe sex positions," I say, not bothering to hide the fact my voice is a little deeper, a little rougher. My mind's stuck on images of her in each position as she takes my cock, all of them ending with her screaming my name. "Early pregnancy can make some women extra horny." I smirk. "You think I haven't noticed how you can't keep your hands off me?"

Her eyes go wide and her cheeks flush that pretty pink that tells me she's turned on. "You've been researching how to fuck me while I'm pregnant?"

"Damn straight." Any nerves I had vanish the second I see how she's responding. Her nipples are already hard against her shirt, and I haven't even touched her yet. "I want to make sure I can still make your legs shake without risking the baby."

She swallows hard. For a split second, I worry I've overstepped, but then she rakes her gaze down my body, biting her lip while she does it. My cock twitches and I know she feels it.

"Show me," she says, voice low and breathy in that I-want-you-inside-me tone.

I pull up the videos I've saved and the first one starts to play. I'm not even watching it. No, all I can think about is trying every one of those positions with Clover's legs wrapped around me and my mouth somewhere on her skin. It plays for all of thirty seconds before she snatches my phone and tosses it onto the nightstand.

"Was that your big request? Showing me some pregnancy kink porn?" She pushes me until I'm flat on my back on the bed and she's crawling over my body.

"Part of it." Because I don't want to just watch it or talk about it. I want to do it all. All the things. Every last one of them until she's wrung out and barely remembers her own name and my balls are empty. Her fingers slip under my shirt and lift it, and I sit up enough to let her strip it over my head.

She drops her head and presses her mouth to my chest, right over my heart, and then trails her tongue down the line of my abs. Fuck, the way she loves them makes all the brutal hours in the gym worth it. I watch her lick and kiss her way across my body, and my cock is so hard it's pushing against the zipper of my jeans trying to get free so it can get in her. But when she tries to undo the button on them, I stop her.

"Get naked," I tell her. "And then get on my face."

Her eyes go so fucking wide. She knows exactly what I want, what I'm asking for. And when she pulls her shirt off and shimmies out of her leggings, I know she wants it too. "I like this request," she says.

"I thought you might," I say, my eyes glued to her tits and the way they sway when she crawls over my body again.

She swings her leg over my head, and I can already smell her. She's soaked. So wet she's already dripping and her pussy hasn't even touched my mouth yet. I'm gripping her hips and pulling her down before she can even straddle my head, and the second her cunt touches my tongue, I'm lost.

She grinds on my face, her body already trembling as I lap at her. I love the sounds she makes when I get my mouth on her, the little gasps and whimpers, the breathy moans that seem to catch in the back of her throat. My hands slide up her thighs, gripping her waist. I hold her down on my tongue, loving the way it feels like she can't help but take what she wants from me.

"Oh god," she whimpers when I suck her clit between my teeth and flick it with the tip of my tongue. "Right there."

My dick's got its own pulse and there's a puddle of pre-cum on my abs, but I need to make her come like this before I fuck her. Need to taste her release in my mouth. Need to feel her gush all over my face. So, I keep working her over, alternating between sucking and licking. Her hands are planted on the headboard, and I can hear her fingernails scraping against the wood. Her legs are shaking just the way I like on either side of my head.

"Banks," she cries out, my name breaking apart in her throat. "I'm gonna come."

Do it, I think, and then she does, and it's so fucking perfect. Her pussy floods my mouth, and I drink it all, licking and sucking her through her orgasm until she's a trembling mess on top of me. She's panting, and I can feel the way her heart is racing against my palm when I slide it up to cup one of her tits.

I roll us, sliding out from beneath her and putting her in front of me so we're spooning, lifting her leg up over my hip. I grip my dick at the base, rubbing it back and forth across her pussy. "Fuck, I wish I could put another baby in you."

Her entire body shudders at my words as my hand slides up to her stomach. Her fingers weave between mine. "Why's that so hot?"

"Because nothing turns me on more than you having my baby." I kiss and lick and run my teeth along her neck as I push inside her. "And after this one comes out, I'm gonna put another one in you," thrust, "and then another one," thrust.

She whimpers as I bottom out inside of her, my cock pressing deep. It feels incredible. Hot and wet and tight and so fucking right. This is where I belong. Inside of her. With her.

"You'd like that, wouldn't you?" I murmur, my mouth right against her ear as I roll my hips into her. "Me knocking you up again and again. Filling this perfect pussy with cum until you get nice and round."

"Banks." My name comes out of her mouth on a gasp. "Fuck, that's so good."

"Maybe I'll put two in there next time," I say, my fingers flexing over her belly. "Twins run in my family."

Her hand reaches behind her, grabbing a handful of my hair. She tugs on it and it sends a jolt of pleasure straight to my balls.

I'm so close. I've been on the edge for what feels like hours. I slide my hand down her stomach and find her clit. "You gonna come again for me?"

"Yes." Her head falls back against my shoulder, pushing her tits out. "God, yes, I'm gonna come."

"Fuck," I groan. My balls tighten up and I know I'm going to come with her as she constricts around me. Her cunt grips me, draining every last drop of cum from my body. I empty myself inside of her, filling her with everything I have as I grind into her, wishing my swimmers could get her pregnant again.

We're both a panting mess, her body limp and boneless in my arms. "So when do you want to try position two?" I ask, brushing her hair off her face.

She just laughs.

Eventually, we move so her body's draped over mine like a

blanket. "Did you mean that?" she asks, her fingers drawing lazy circles on my chest.

"Mean what?"

"About putting another baby in me?" Her eyes flicker up to mine, and I can see the faintest hint of pink on her cheeks.

"I did." I slide my hand over her stomach. "If you want to, when this one's out."

"Yeah," she whispers. "Yeah, I do. I want all your babies."

I can't help but smile because I didn't know how much I needed to hear her say that until she did. "Good." I slide my fingers between her thighs and find her still soaking with my cum so I press it back inside of her. "Because I'm gonna keep trying until we have an entire baseball team's worth."

Her laughter is the most perfect sound I've ever heard.

She's quiet for a minute after that, her fingers tracing random patterns on my chest. Then she asks, "Do you think we should tell people soon? About the baby?"

The question catches me off guard, but only because I've been thinking about the same damn thing. "Yeah, I think we need to. Especially Kasen." My stomach twists just saying his name. I've been avoiding my best friend because I wasn't sure when she'd want to tell him and I'm a shitty liar. "He needs to hear it from us before anyone else finds out."

I feel her whole body go rigid against mine at the mention of her brother. "He's going to completely lose his shit."

"One hundred percent," I agree, because there's no point lying to her. "He's gonna want to kill me. Probably will try." I run my hand down her back, feeling her relax slightly under my touch. "But he'll get over it eventually. He loves you more than anything. And he's my best friend. We've been through worse."

That might be a lie. We definitely haven't been through me knocking up his little sister.

She sighs and presses closer, her head tucked under my chin. "I'm glad it's you, Banks. That you're here with me."

It's not "I love you," but it's something. Something real. And for now, it's enough. I pull her tighter against me, still amazed that this stubborn, control-freak of a woman has completely upended my entire life in the best possible way.

"Where else would I be, Freckles?" I whisper into her hair. "This is exactly where I belong."

I'll tell her I love her soon. But tonight, with her falling asleep in my arms and our baby growing inside her, I don't need to say the words out loud. They're right there in every beat of my heart.

18
Clover

"HE'S GOING to kill you, then me, then you again."

Banks just laughs, adjusting the collar of his button-down shirt in my bedroom mirror while I maneuver Mai Tai around on the floor so she catches the best light. "A little dramatic, don't you think, Freckles?"

"It's Kasen we're talking about. Remember that time he threatened to break some poor dude's legs for just asking me to prom?" I ignore the storm clouds rolling across Banks's face at the memory. I forgot he was right there with my brother making those threats.

I smooth my dress down over my barely there twelve-week baby bump—it's just a small, firm curve that most people would probably just mistake for me eating one of those giant Chipotle burritos. "Now we're about to tell him that his best friend knocked up his little sister. So no, I really don't think I'm being dramatic at all."

Three freaking months. That's how long this tiny human has been growing inside me. Three months since that thunderstorm changed everything. A whole month since Banks found out and point-blank refused to go back to his own apartment, despite Kasen's increasingly confused questions about why he was still basically living on my couch. Not that Banks has slept on the couch even once since finding out about the baby.

Honestly, it's a straight-up miracle we've managed to make it this long without Kasen somehow figuring out about the baby.

Banks comes up behind me, wrapping those strong firefighter arms of his around my waist. His hands settle right on my stomach, all protective and possessive in a way that still manages to make my knees go weak every time.

"Let him try," Banks murmurs, his lips brushing against my ear and sending shivers down my spine. "I'm not going anywhere, Freckles."

I roll my eyes at the nickname he refuses to drop, but secretly I love it. Not that I'd ever tell him that. His ego is already big enough.

"Your funeral," I mutter, leaning back against his chest. "Just so you know, I'm not visiting you in the hospital."

"Liar," he says, pressing a quick kiss to the side of my neck, right where it meets my shoulder. "You'd be the first one there, probably yelling at the nurses for not giving me enough pain meds."

The worst part is, he's one hundred percent right about that. When the hell did he start knowing me better than I even know myself?

Forty minutes later, we're walking through the front door of Timber, my brother's pride and joy. The microbrewery is packed for a Thursday night, the warm glow of Edison bulbs casting everything in a flattering light. The smell of hops and barley hits me like a truck, and I swallow hard against the immediate wave of nausea and the mouth full of saliva that comes along with it.

Banks's hand finds the small of my back and I lean back a little into the warmth of him. "You okay?"

"Fine," I lie, ignoring the way my stomach is launching a full-scale rebellion despite the peppermint I've been sucking on or the ginger tea I choked down before we came. "Let's get this over with."

Kasen's eyes land on us as soon as we walk in, and his eyebrows shoot up in genuine surprise as we approach the bar. I take a deep breath that doesn't help at all and plaster on my best *everything's totally normal and I'm not about to ruin your whole day* smile.

"Can't say I expected to see you two together today. Everything alright?" He gives Banks a questioning look before turning his attention to me, already moving in for one of his bone-crushing hugs that squeezes my stomach. There's a very real possibility I'm about to barf on my brother's shoes, but I somehow manage to swallow it back.

"Yeah, everything's fine," I manage to say, but my voice comes out a little squeaky.

My brother frowns at me, but then he and Banks do that ridiculous handshake-turned-bro-hug thing that makes me want to roll my eyes into the back of my head. *Men.*

Kasen leads us over to a booth in the back and sits down.

His eyes narrow as Banks and I slide into the same side of the booth across from him, his gaze darting suspiciously between us. His fingers drum against the wooden table, and his tattoos shift on his forearm with the movement. It's a little hypnotizing to be honest. I've always thought they were cool, the full sleeves of colorful ink that peek out from beneath his rolled-up flannel, continuing up his neck in a riot of colors that clash with the black beanie he's perpetually wearing over his messy dark hair.

I'm not brave enough to get my own, but I sort of wish I was.

"Okay, what's going on?" he asks, startling me out of my runaway thoughts. "You call me sounding all serious about needing to talk, and then you show up with him?" He nods toward Banks. "Not that I'm complaining about seeing my two favorite people, but you two arriving together when you've been acting weird for weeks... Something's up."

I glance at Banks, and he must read the panic on my face because he grabs my hand and threads our fingers together. Now that the time has come to spill our secret, the words are just... gone. We've spent hours this past week planning exactly how to do this. But sitting here across from my overprotective brother, whose suspicion is only getting worse by the second.

"We have some news," Banks says, rescuing me from my sudden muteness. He squeezes my hand, tightening his grip and I squeeze him right back to let him know I appreciate him doing this with me. For me.

Whatever.

Kasen looks between Banks and me again. "The two of you have news," he repeats, his voice flat. He leans back, crossing his arms like he's bracing for something. "Okay..."

"Clover's pregnant," Banks says, and how is his voice so steady? I swallow down the bile creeping up the back of my throat "We're having a baby."

Yep.

He just said that.

Out loud.

Kasen's face goes through about fifteen different emotions in five seconds—shock, confusion, disbelief, and finally, something that looks a whole lot like murderous rage.

"You're what?" he finally manages, his voice dangerously quiet.

"Pregnant," I repeat as I finally find my voice. "Twelve weeks along."

Kasen's gaze swings to Banks, who hasn't flinched once. "You got my sister pregnant? After I asked you to look out for her? And then hid it from me for fucking *weeks*?"

Banks meets my brother's glare head-on. "Yes."

"This isn't how we planned to tell you," I jump in, because I can read the look on my brother's face and he's about to jump over this table and strangle his best friend. "We've only known for a little while and needed time to process it ourselves. But we're telling you now because we wanted you to hear it from us before anyone else."

"So you've been keeping this from me this whole time? While we've all been hanging out like nothing's changed?" Kasen's voice is tight with hurt beneath the anger.

"It's not what you think," I start, but Banks cuts me off.

"I'm in love with her."

Wait, what?

My head whips around so fast I get a little dizzy. Banks's eyes are locked on Kasen, his jaw set in that stubborn way of his. The man thinks *I'm* the stubborn one, but he gives me a run for my money.

"Excuse me?" my brother says, and oh man. His voice has this deadly quiet to it. That's when you know he's big time angry. Not when he's yelling but when he gets like this.

"You heard me," Banks says like he didn't just drop a nuclear bomb on me in the middle of my brother's brewery. " I love your sister, Kase. Have for years. And I know you're pissed, but Clover's it for me. Her and our baby. I'm not going anywhere, no matter how you feel about it."

My heart is trying to break out of my chest it's beating so hard. *Banks loves me?* Since when? And why the hell is he telling my brother before telling me?

Kasen's expression is unreadable. Then, without warning, he stands up and points at Banks then toward the door. "Outside. Now."

"Kasen—" I start to protest.

"It's okay," Banks says, squeezing my hand before sliding out of the booth. "We'll be right back."

I watch in horrified fascination as my brother and the

father of my child march out the front door of the brewery. Through Timber's windows, I watch them facing off on the sidewalk—Kasen gesturing wildly, face flushed with anger, while Banks stands like an immovable object, arms crossed over his chest, nodding occasionally.

"Why are men the worst?" I mutter to myself, digging around in my purse to find another mint. It doesn't help and my eyes water with the effort not to throw up. "I'm a grown-ass woman who can have a baby with whoever I want, for fuck's sake."

I'll light a candle for whoever my brother decides to procreate with. He's such a caveman, the poor girl's going to need all the help she can get.

I'm sure I look like a crazy person talking to myself, so to feel less crazy, I pull my phone out and start scrolling through my socials.

When five minutes turn into ten, I start wondering whether I'll need to dip into my bar fund to bail both of them out of jail tonight. But just as I'm about to go out there and tear them both a new one for being alphahole idiots, they walk back through the door. Kasen still looks pissy, but it's not as bad as it was when they left. Banks's jaw looks a little swollen on one side but his eyes are soft when he slides into the booth beside me and grabs my hand.

"So," my brother says, sliding into the booth like he never left. If it wasn't for his swollen knuckles and the tightness in his jaw, I'd think he was almost happy. "I'm going to be an uncle."

As much as his display a minute ago annoyed me, seeing him now, ready to accept my baby, and his role in its life, is everything. I didn't dare hope in my wildest dreams this would happen today. And just like that, I'm fighting back tears. *Again.* Stupid pregnancy hormones. "Yeah, you are. And while I'm sorry we didn't tell you sooner, I'm not sorry for how I handled it. We were trying to figure things out first—

without the testosterone-fueled showdown I knew would happen."

Kasen reaches across the table and takes my hand. "That's fair. I'm still pissed you kept this from me, but I'll get over it." Then he shoots a look at Banks that could turn a lesser man to stone. "And if he doesn't treat you right, or keeps anything else from me, I'll still break his face."

I yank my hand away. "Oh for fuck's sake. I don't need you to threaten violence on my behalf. I'm perfectly capable of breaking his face myself if necessary."

"I'd expect nothing less," Banks replies, wrapping his arm around me and kissing the top of my head. "But it won't be necessary."

The look he gives me is so sure, so full of whatever emotion made him say he loves me out loud to my brother before saying it to me, that I momentarily forget I'm annoyed with him. Almost.

"You better have a ring ready," Kasen grumbles.

"Excuse me?" I snap back to reality with a vengeance. "Nobody said anything about marriage. Did you two work out my dowry while you were out there too? How many goats am I worth these days?"

"You're having his baby!"

"Welcome to the twenty-first century, Kasen. People have babies without getting married all the time. It's almost like women have autonomy over their own lives now."

"But—"

"Trust me, I've tried talking to her about it," Banks says, and I elbow him hard in the side. He grunts but grins at my brother. "She's stubborn."

"And you both have traumatic brain injuries if you think my reproductive choices automatically lead to a wedding," I say loud enough for them both to hear, but of course they act like I'm not even here.

Honestly? I'm feeling a little stabby, not gonna lie.

"She gets that from our Mom," Kasen sighs. But then his eyes light up. "Jesus. I'm going to be an uncle." His whole face transforms with the first genuine smile since we sat down. "That kid's gonna have the most badass uncle. I'll teach him all sorts of shit and then give him back."

"She's going to be a girl," Banks says confidently. "And you're not teaching her shit unless you run it by me first."

I roll my eyes so hard I'm surprised they don't get stuck looking at my brain. "So glad you two have my child's entire future mapped out already."

"It's a he," Kasen argues, continuing to ignore me. "James' make sons. It's genetic."

"Actually, the father determines the sex of the baby," I point out, "because sperm carry either an X or Y chromosome, while eggs only carry X chromosomes. So if anyone's going to make bold proclamations about our baby's gender, it should be me. Or Banks."

They both stare at me.

"What? I've been reading."

Kasen shakes his head and signals one of his servers. "I need a beer for this conversation."

"Make it two," I add, then smile sweetly at their shocked expressions. "Relax, it's for you," I tell Banks. "You're going to need it when I explain exactly how I feel about you planning my future without me."

⛈

Telling the rest of our inner circle goes significantly better than telling Kasen.

Navy meets us at Ember after her shift with a knowing smirk. "So you finally told big brother about the bun in the oven?" she asks, giving Banks an appraising look. "And you're still breathing. That's unexpected."

"He's tougher than he looks," I reply, which makes Banks raise an eyebrow.

She pulls me into a tight hug. "I'm so glad you two are finally going public with this. Now I can officially start planning the baby shower!" She bounces on her toes. "I'm thinking a midnight garden theme with tiny fairy lights and fireflies. And don't worry, I'll make sure everything is put into our shared calendar with your planning system so you don't stress."

She's already talking about godmother duties and food choices for the shower before I've even had a chance to sit down.

My boss's reaction is more reserved but no less supportive. "I had a feeling," Theo says, looking between us with a smirk. "The way Banks has been hanging around the bar like your bodyguard every night made me suspect something was up."

Banks shrugs, completely unapologetic and owning his hovering. He guides me to the barstool he's insisting I sit on instead of standing and waits for me to sit before moving behind me so I can use his chest to lean back against.

Theo smirks at me and I bite back a laugh. Banks might've backed off a tiny bit, but he's still over the top with everything related to me or the baby.

The fire station crew is the most entertaining reaction by far. They erupt into a combination of merciless teasing and overprotectiveness for a baby they haven't even met, and it makes me cry a little. Banks gets endless shit, but he loves every second of it.

"Priestly, settling down?" Captain Morgan's bushy eyebrows lift up so his forehead wrinkles. "Never thought I'd see the day."

"Pay up," Brenna says, holding out her hand to Martinez and Vetter who bitch and groan before they hand their cash over.

"You were betting on us?" I ask, equal parts horrified and amused.

"Babe, we've had a betting pool since Banks had a panic attack when he didn't know where you were during that gas leak," Brenna explains with a knowing smirk. "He came back to the station going on and on about how you were basically superwoman after, and Martinez said he'd never seen anyone crush so hard over emergency management skills. Only question was how long it'd take you two to get your shit together and figure it out."

And through every minute of telling our friends and family, Banks is right there beside me, his arm thrown over my shoulders so he can pull me into him. He's always like this now, touching me all the time. The man doesn't know the meaning of keeping his hands to himself. He's steadfast. His presence in my life is unwavering.

What isn't unwavering, however, is my traitor of a body, which seems determined to remind me daily that this pregnancy isn't going to be the glowing, Instagram-worthy experience some women claim it is.

19
Clover

IT HAPPENS on a particularly busy Friday night at Ember, three weeks after telling everyone our news. The nausea has been relentless all day, and the meds Dr. Walker gave me aren't doing shit. Well, it's really 24/7 sickness with very few breaks, but I've been forcing myself to function through sheer willpower and an ungodly amount of ginger candies, mint, and a set of Sea Bands that I swear do nothing but I'm too afraid to take off because what if it really is worse without them?

Navy keeps shooting me worried looks that I hate as I mix drinks with shaking hands, stopping every few minutes to take deep breaths and steady myself when the room starts spinning.

Yeah, not being able to hold anything down for days is starting to catch up with me.

"You need to go home," she says for at least the tenth time since I clocked in. "You look like death again, and not in a sexy vampire way."

"I'm fine," I lie, even as I grip the edge of the bar to keep from swaying. "Just need to make it through the rush."

But my body has other plans. One moment I'm reaching for a bottle of tequila, and the next, the entire world tilts sideways. A cold sweat breaks out across my forehead, my vision tunnels, and I realize with distant horror that I'm about to pass out.

Navy grabs me by the elbow before I hit the ground and somehow I manage to get my feet back under me. The bottle isn't so lucky and it smashes to the floor. I don't even have enough energy to care that everyone's staring. "Nope. That's it. Office. Now."

She practically drags me to the back since I can barely hold myself up, and when we get there, she shoves me in Theo's office chair. I lean forward and put my head between my knees while black and silver spots pop in front of my eyes. The room is spinning so fast there's a good chance I'll throw up from the vertigo alone.

If I had anything in my system to throw up.

"I'm calling Banks," she says, already pulling out her phone.

"Don't you dare." I try to sound intimidating or commanding or whatever, but it comes out as almost a whisper which isn't helping my case. "He'll just worry."

"He *should* worry. You're not okay."

"I'm fine. I just need a minute."

Navy ignores me, putting her phone up to her ear. You know it's bad when she's making an actual phone call instead of texting. "Hey, you need to come get her. She's being a stubborn ass and refusing to go home but she almost passed out." My best friend glares at me. "It was scary and she looks like she's two seconds away from death. Okay. Yeah. Hurry."

The next twenty minutes pass in a blur of nausea and dizziness and I'm pretty sure I lose consciousness a few times. My forehead rests on Theo's desk, and I vaguely register Navy forcing me to sip water. It sloshes in my stomach in a gross way, and I doubt it'll stay down.

There's the sound of concerned voices around me but I'm too weak and exhausted to care or try to figure out what they're saying. It all feels like it's happening underwater until a new voice breaks through the haze.

"Clover." Banks is suddenly there, kneeling in front of me, his hands cupping my face and lifting my head so I can look at him but my eyes roll around in my skull and the water starts creeping up the back of my throat. A cold sweat breaks out across my forehead and down my back but I try to give him a smile. I don't think it works because the fear in his eyes is so intense it hurts to look at him. "Jesus Christ, baby."

"I'm fine," I mumble, though it's obviously the biggest lie I've ever told. "Just need a minute."

"Fuck that." He scoops me up like I weigh nothing, cradling me against his chest. He's strong, but I've also lost a ton of weight. All I know is I'm glad he's got me, because I don't think I could walk out of here even if my life depended on it. "I'm taking you to the ER. We're done doing this your way."

I want to protest, to insist that I can walk, that I don't need to be carried out of my own bar like some fainting damsel. But I'm so tired and sick and dizzy that all I can do is press my face into his neck and breathe in the comforting smell of him. It's the only thing that's calmed my stomach in hours.

"It's okay," he whispers against my hair, his voice steadier than his racing heartbeat under my ear. "I've got you."

Half an hour later, we're sitting in Dr. Walker's office instead of the ER after he agreed to meet us when Banks texted him. Since I hate hospitals, this is so much better. As much as I don't want to admit it, the IV fluids they've got me hooked up to are already making me feel more human-like and less like a cave troll.

The room isn't spinning anymore so I'm calling it a win.

"Hyperemesis gravidarum," Dr. Walker confirms as he walks into the room, looking at my chart with a concerned frown. "It's severe morning sickness that can lead to dehydration and weight loss if left untreated. You've lost five pounds since your last visit, which is concerning at this stage of pregnancy. And do we need to talk about how bad you let the dehydration get before you called me?"

I shift my eyes away because I'm feeling guilty as hell. I didn't want to admit my failure as a mother, so I made everything worse by not asking for help. And in the end, it wasn't even me who made the call, it was Banks.

I blink back tears as I glance up at him. He's going to be such a good dad.

Banks's hand tightens around mine. "What do we do?" The fear in his voice makes me feel even more like a failure than I already do.

"We'll start a different, stronger medication to control the nausea," Dr. Walker explains. "And I strongly recommend reducing your work hours, especially time spent on your feet. Rest is crucial right now, as is staying hydrated."

"What?" The shitty thing about having a little more energy is now I've got the ability to panic. And sure enough, I start to go into panic mode thinking about everything I'm going to fall behind on and whether or not I'll ever be able to make it all up. "But I can't—the bar needs me, and I have finals coming up, and—"

"Clover." Dr. Walker's voice is gentle but firm. "I understand you have responsibilities, but right now, your primary responsibility is to yourself and your baby. Your body is telling you it needs rest."

I slump back against the exam table, defeated. Banks's thumb traces circles on the back of my hand, and focusing on that is the only thing keeping me from bursting into tears.

Dr. Walker asks us to stop by his office once the nurse removes my IV and gives me the all-clear. We follow her down the hallway to a fancy office with a desk buried under all kinds of books and paperwork. Honestly, it's kind of a mess.

The view is spectacular, though. And the leather couch in

here looks overstuffed and soft and I'm tempted to lay down and take a nap. All my muscles ache like the day after that time I tried Pilates, and every time I blink it gets harder to open my eyes.

Thank all that's holy for Banks because he's the only thing keeping me upright.

As Dr. Walker prints out some information sheets for us, I notice the small flatscreen mounted on the wall silently playing highlights from last night's Trailblazers game. The stack of takeout menus peeking out from under his desk calendar doesn't escape my notice either.

The guy kind of seems like he lives here, especially since it's almost midnight on a Friday night and he was here and ready to help us within half an hour.

"You a basketball fan?" Banks asks, following my gaze to the TV.

Dr. Walker glances up, a flicker of surprise crossing his face at the personal question. "Yeah, actually. Been following the Blazers since residency. Helps me decompress after long shifts." He hands me the prescription with a slightly embarrassed smile.

"They're playing Sunday," Banks says. "A bunch of us are getting together at Timber—her brother's brewery—to watch. You should stop by if you're not delivering babies or whatever."

I raise an eyebrow at Banks, but honestly, it's not the worst idea. Dr. Walker seems to be about Banks's age and looking around his office, he seems lonely. Or at the very least married to his job. He's also kind of awkward when he's not talking about medical stuff.

Dr. Walker hesitates, but then a small smile lights up his face. "I might just do that. I've been watching too many games alone in this office lately."

"First round's on the house," I offer, surprising myself. "I know the owner."

That small smile turns to a full-on grin. "I'll hold you to that. But only if you promise to follow my instructions." He taps the printed sheets. "Medicine. Rest. Hydration. Doctor's orders."

I agree and then Banks helps me out to the car. The ride home is quiet, with Banks shooting worried glances at me every few seconds while I stare out the window. After the IV I feel better, but I don't know how to process the way my body's failing me.

Once we're back in my apartment, the dam finally breaks.

"I can't do this," I whisper, sinking onto the couch as tears start falling. It's a whole downpour and I can't stop it. "I'm going to be a horrible mom," I sob, barely able to get the words out. "Our baby's going to struggle because I can't take care of it."

Banks is beside me in a blink, pulling me into his lap and cradling me against his chest like a baby. Can't say I hate it. "Hey, no. That's not true."

"It is true!" The sob that tears out of me is ugly and raw. "I'm failing at the most basic thing I'm supposed to be able to do. Grow a healthy baby. And now I have to cut back at work, which means less money saved for my bar, and I'll probably fail my finals because I can't stay awake long enough to study—"

"Shh," Banks murmurs, his fingers running through my hair. "You're not failing at anything. Your body's working overtime to grow our kid. That's not failure, Freckles. That's strength."

"But my plans—"

"We'll adjust them." He pulls back just enough to look me in the eye. "I've already been working on some ideas."

Before I can ask what he means, he's setting me on the couch beside him and getting up, grabbing his laptop. He returns and pulls up a spreadsheet that looks suspiciously like something I'd make.

"So, I mapped out your class schedule and put together a study plan that works around when you typically feel best during the day," he explains, pointing to the screen. "I've also worked out my shifts so I can take you to class when you're too sick to drive, and pick up more of the household stuff so you can rest. Navy and Kasen agreed to help out, too. Navy's going to pick up more of your hours and Kase's going to be backup for anything I can't be here for. Plus, he's gonna water your plants."

I stare at him, at this incredible man who knows me so well and who's done this amazing thing I never would've asked him to do. This spreadsheet he's created just for me, the way he's rearranged his life around mine, and something in me just crumbles. Just gives way to the avalanche of feelings I've been trying to hold back.

"You did this for me?" My voice comes out embarrassingly small.

His eyes go all melty. "Of course I did. We're a team, remember? You're not doing any of this alone. You're the strongest person I know, but that doesn't mean you don't need help."

Maybe he's right, and he's earned my trust.

So I give in.

Slowly, reluctantly, I start to lean on him. For the first time in my life, I let someone else take some of the weight. It terrifies me how easy it becomes over the next week—falling asleep on his chest while studying, waking to find he's highlighted passages in my textbook and left sticky notes with helpful summaries.

One night, I'm crying over a low grade on a quiz (stupid pregnancy hormones) and I can't stop. But Banks shows up yet again. He holds me through the night, his lips pressed against my hair as he whispers promises I'm afraid to believe.

Despite myself, I'm starting to believe them. I'm starting to believe in *him*.

"You don't have to do everything alone anymore," he murmurs into the darkness. "That's what I'm here for."

Now I'm lying awake, watching him sleep beside me. His face is softer in sleep, younger somehow without the weight of responsibility he carries during the day. One of his hands rests protectively over my small but growing bump, a habit he's developed that melts something inside me every time.

I trace the outline of his stubbled jaw with my eyes, remembering what he said to Kasen. *I'm in love with her. I've been in love with her for years.*

He still hasn't said those words to me directly, and I haven't said them back. Because what if this is all just obligation? What if he's only here, only doing all of this, because of our baby? What if I let myself believe this could be forever, only to have him realize he never signed up for this?

His hand twitches on my stomach in his sleep, like he's already protecting our child from my doubts.

And that's when it hits me, with a clarity that steals my breath. I'm falling in love with Banks Priestly. Actually, if I'm being completely honest with myself—which is something I try to avoid at all costs—I've been falling for him since that first night during the thunderstorm.

Or maybe I've been falling for him since I was a teenager.

But one thing's for sure: I'm in love with him, and I'm terrified.

Because this feels a lot like I've unexpectedly stumbled into my own ever after when I'm barely ready for right now.

20
Banks

IT'S BEEN two weeks since Clover nearly collapsed at Ember, and I'm still a fucking wreck every time she so much as yawns.

"Seriously, Priestly. Take a breath before you pass out." Brenna flops onto the bench next to me in the station gym, blonde curls yanked into that tight ponytail she always wears on shift. "You've been staring at your phone for twenty minutes. Pretty sure it'll buzz if something important happens."

I grunt and shove my phone into my pocket, forcing my attention to the free weights. "Just checking the time."

"Bullshit." She snags a pair of fifteens and starts on bicep curls, eyeing me in the mirror. "You're checking to make sure your pregnant girlfriend hasn't spontaneously combusted in the last five minutes."

"She's not my girlfriend," I mutter—though, let's be real, that's basically exactly what Clover is. We live together, share a bed, split a baby fund, and I'm a thousand percent in love with her. But we haven't slapped any official label on it, and it's starting to eat at me.

"Right." Brenna rolls her eyes. "You just knocked her up,

moved in, and look at her like she could chop off your leg and you'd thank her for it."

"It's complicated." I grab the thirties and hammer out a set of curls, trying to channel my frustration somewhere useful. "She's different, all right? Independent as hell. Doesn't want to need anybody."

"And that's a problem because...?"

"Because I want her to need me," I bite out. "Not just as the father of her kid. I want her to—hell, I want to be everything to her."

Brenna sets her weights aside and gives me a pointed look. "Have you told her that?"

"Not in so many words."

"Then how the hell is she supposed to know?"

I shrug, racking the dumbbells with more force than necessary. "Not exactly. But I told her brother I'm in love with her. Right in front of her."

"That's not the same as telling her, dumbass." She shakes her head like I'm a rookie who can't find the hose. "She doesn't want your protection, Banks. She wants your honesty. She wants to know she's a choice you'd make every day even without the baby."

Her words nail me in the chest, stripping away all my lame excuses. Brenna's always had a talent for slicing through my bullshit.

"Let me guess," Brenna continues when I don't respond. "You're so focused on taking care of her and the baby that you've forgotten to actually show her who you really are as a partner—who you want to be for her."

"What's that even mean?" I grab a towel, wiping the sweat off my forehead, buying time because her words have cut open something uncomfortable in my chest.

"I mean that you're so worried about being the perfect baby daddy that you're not showing her the man who wants to build a life with her." Brenna stands and pokes me hard in the chest. "Show her who you really are, not who you think she wants you to be."

The station alarm blares before I can respond, sending us both sprinting toward the bay for a medical call. But Brenna's words follow me the rest of the shift, digging under my skin like splinters.

Show her who you really are.

By the time I clock out the next morning, I know exactly what I need to do.

When I pull up to the house in the Sellwood neighborhood for the second time, my palms are sweating against the steering wheel. This is a big fucking step, probably the biggest I've ever taken. I'm more nervous about this than I've ever been stepping into a fire.

"Are you sure about this?" The realtor, a no-nonsense woman named Ellen, shoots me a sideways glance from the passenger seat. "It's a big commitment, especially without your partner here."

"I'm sure." I unbuckle and swing out of the truck, my eyes fixing on the navy blue house with its wide front porch and white oak tree in the front yard that's perfect for a swing. The 'For Sale' sign still sits in the front yard, but if everything goes according to plan today, it won't be there much longer. "She'll love it."

I hope.

Two hours later, I've scrawled my name on about a thousand forms, handed over the biggest down payment check of my life, and now I'm staring at keys in my palm. My hands won't stop shaking.

"Congratulations, Mr. Priestly." She shakes my hand with a firm grip. "The sellers are thrilled with the quick close—you can move in immediately."

I thank her, but my gaze stays fixed on the place that's now mine. Ours, if Clover will have it. The house we'll raise our kids in, if she says yes. "I really appreciate you pulling this together so fast."

"Not a problem. Let me know if you need any recommendations for movers or contractors for the modifications you mentioned."

I nod, but my mind's already buzzing with possibilities: the nursery in that upstairs room with the bay window that will fit so many of Clover's plants, an office for her across the hall, a fenced yard out back for summer BBQs. I can see it all. The bones of this place feel like the start of something huge.

Now all I need is for Clover to feel it, too.

"Where are we going?" Clover shifts in my truck's passenger seat, one hand resting on the small but definite baby bump now visible beneath her sweater. She's sixteen weeks along now, and the hyperemesis has finally started to ease, though she still has rough days. "You know how I feel about surprises."

"You hate them," I acknowledge, reaching across the console to squeeze her hand. "But you'll like this one. Promise."

"That's what you said about the 'pregnancy superfood smoothie' you made me last week, and I threw it up all over the bathroom floor."

"Low blow, Freckles." I grimace at the memory. The kale-and-beet nightmare was not my finest moment in pregnancy nutrition. "This is better than a smoothie."

She arches an eyebrow, still wary as hell. "It better be. I'm skipping a nap for this."

The fact that she's admitting she needs a nap is progress. A month ago, she'd have rather died than acknowledge any weakness. Hyperemesis, however, doesn't really give her a choice.

All I can do is hope that what's waiting at the end of this drive is enough to show her exactly who I am—and exactly how serious I am about our future.

I turn onto the quiet, tree-lined street, and my pulse skyrockets. This is it—the moment of truth.

"Close your eyes," I say as we near the house.

She shoots me a wary look. "Banks—"

"Please? Just for thirty seconds."

With a long-suffering sigh I've come to find adorable instead of irritating, she closes her eyes. "This better not be another baby thing. If you've ordered more—"

"It's not." I pull into the driveway and cut the engine. My stomach feels like it's hosting a circus, and I take an extra second to breathe before hopping out. "Keep 'em closed. No peeking."

I circle around to her side, open the door, and help her out of the truck. Her hand grips mine as I guide her up the stone path to the front porch. The early spring air is crisp, carrying the scent of newly bloomed flowers from the garden beds I've spent the past week filling with perennials.

I know how she feels about her plants.

"Okay," I say once we're at the perfect spot, my hands on her shoulders. Fuck, I hope she likes it. "Open."

Her eyes snap open, those pretty blue eyes of hers that I hope the baby has widening as she takes in the house in front of us. The fresh navy blue paint with white trim. The big front porch I could see us rocking in chairs on when we're old.

"What is this?" Her voice is so soft I almost don't catch it. "One of your firefighter buddies' places or something?"

My heart's about to bust right out of my chest. "It's ours," I say, the words nearly sticking in my throat. "If you want it to be."

Her head whips around so fast I'm surprised she doesn't hurt herself. "What?"

"I bought it," I say, fishing the keys from my pocket with fingers that won't stop shaking. The metal catches the sun, throwing light across her shocked face. "For us. For our family."

"You bought a house?" Her voice climbs higher with each word, her eyes going wide. "Without telling me? Without even asking me? Banks, what the actual fuck?"

Yeah, I was braced for that reaction—this is Clover, after all. She's not the type to squeal and leap into my arms. She's going to tear this apart, piece by piece, before she accepts it might be a good idea. Honestly, it's one of the things I love about her—that sharp brain that never lets her take the easy route.

"Just look at it before you tear me a new one," I say, catching her hand and leading her to the door. "Please?"

She goes quiet, those blue eyes drilling into mine like she's trying to dismantle me piece by piece. Christ, I'd let her if she wanted to. Finally, she nods once. "Fine. Show me."

The key slides home with a satisfying click, and I push the door open. The entryway opens up with hardwood floors that gleam in the afternoon light pouring through the windows. The place is practically glowing, like it's been waiting for her to walk through the door.

"It's four bedrooms, two baths," I rattle off as she steps inside. "Built over a century ago but fully renovated five years back—new roof, plumbing, electrical. The foundation's reinforced for earthquakes, so it's not going anywhere."

I sound like a desperate realtor, but I can't help it. I need her to know I didn't just throw money at the first house I saw. That I checked every damn detail because this is where I want us to raise our kids. Where I want to come home to her after every shift.

Clover glides through the living room, her fingers brushing the built-ins around the old brick fireplace. Her face shifts, that initial shock melting into something softer—something that makes my chest tighten with hope.

"The kitchen's back here," I say, setting a hand on the small of her back to guide her. "I figured you'd want to see that first."

The minute I first walked in, I knew this kitchen was perfect for her: big and modern while still rocking that vintage feel—white subway tile, blue-gray cabinets, brass pulls, and a deep farmhouse sink under a window overlooking the backyard.

"There's a garden window for all your plant babies," I add, pointing it out. "Manhattan and Mint Julep will like that morning sun, but the moody ones—Old Fashioned and the rest—can sit on the shaded shelf."

She spins toward me, eyes wide. For a second, I think I've messed up big-time.

"You remember which ones need indirect light?" she asks, voice catching.

"'Course I do," I shrug, trying to play it cool even though my heart's pounding. "I pay attention to the things that matter to you."

She huffs a laugh, but it sounds suspiciously close to a sob. Her gaze skims over the window ledge, and I can only imagine what's going through her head. When she turns back to me, there's something in her eyes I haven't seen before—some soft mix of gratitude and wonder that makes my chest tighten.

I clear my throat, shifting gears because I'm not sure I can handle her tears right now—especially not if they're happy ones. "Anyway," I say, leading her deeper into the kitchen, my hand at the small of her back. "Check this out."

I lead her farther into the kitchen, running a hand over the counters. "There's tons of space for when you're stress-baking."

I open the pantry door to reveal the spice rack I installed last night. "Check it out—ready to be alphabetized just how you like it even if it makes zero fucking sense to organize them that way."

She lets out this half-laugh, half-sob sound that twists my insides. "Banks..."

"Come on. There's more." I tug her gently toward the stairs, showing off the updated bathroom with hex tiles and a vintage clawfoot tub I immediately pictured her in, surrounded by bubbles.

The best part is it's big enough to fit us both.

I push open the door to the smallest bedroom. "This would be your office. Until you get your bar up and running."

The space is bare except for the desk I had delivered a few days ago—a midcentury piece I found at an estate sale. I spent three nights refinishing it while Clover was working. My hands still smell like wood polish. I positioned it right under the window with the best view of the backyard.

"I know you need space that's all yours," I tell her, watching her face. "Somewhere to work or study without me hovering or the baby crying."

She runs her fingers over the desktop, and even though she's silent, I can see all the little tells that say she's feeling something big.

"This next one's the nursery," I say, leading her across the hall. "Morning sun comes right in, and it's close to the master so we'll hear the baby. And it's the perfect place for Bellini."

The walls are painted a pale green—neutral, but still cozy. I've already set up the crib I spent weeks researching, and above it hangs a mobile with clouds and lightning bolts and tiny raindrops. When the light catches them, they sparkle like bits of magic.

It's more than a house—it's the foundation of the life I want with her.

"The mobile felt right," I say, breaking the silence when she just stands there. "I know we haven't talked about a theme yet, but it reminded me of that night. The storm."

The night everything changed—the night we made this baby and I stopped trying to bury my feelings for Clover James.

She lifts a hand to cover her mouth, tears building in her eyes. Aw, hell. This is way too much, too fast. I swore I wouldn't push her, and here I am, practically bulldozing her into a future she hasn't even agreed to.

"You don't have to decide anything right now," I blurt, taking a step back. "The house is mine regardless—I already gave up my apartment. But it only becomes ours if you want it to be."

Her voice comes out thick. "What's in there?" She nods toward the last closed door at the end of the hall. She's fighting tears like a champ, but I know my girl—she's close to breaking.

"Master bedroom."

Before I can stop her, she's pushing past me, shoving the door open. The space is huge, with bay windows and a built-in window seat I immediately pictured her curled up in. There's no bed yet, but I strung lights along the ceiling—soft, warm ones that won't kill our eyes when the baby's screaming at three in the morning.

"I thought it might help," I offer, feeling more exposed than I have in years. "You know, when the baby's up all night...these lights will be easier than the overhead."

Clover turns to face me, and there's no hiding the tears sliding down her cheeks now. "Why are you doing all this?" she whispers.

This is it. No more hiding.

"Because I'm in love with you," I tell her, the words feeling like they've been trapped in my chest for years. "Not because of the baby. Not because we're living together. I've been falling for you since you were seventeen, and I'm done pretending otherwise."

I move into her space, backing her against the doorframe. My arms cage her in as I lower my face to hers.

Her lips part, and I can see the shock on her face. I should have done this a long time ago instead of telling her brother first like an idiot.

"I know I messed up," I admit, leaning in. "Telling Kasen I was in love with you before I ever said it to your face wasn't my best move. You deserved to hear it from me first." I cradle her face, swiping tears away with my thumbs. "I've waited too long for you, Freckles. I've held back, kept my distance, let you set the pace. But I'm done waiting. This isn't about obligation—it's about us. Building something real together. I want all of it—this house, our family, coming home to you, waking up beside you every morning. I'd collapse every bridge, burn every map, break every compass—just to be the only way home you'll ever need. You're mine, Clover—both of you are."

She breathes my name, so soft it nearly breaks me. "I'm so scared," she confesses, voice trembling.

"Of what?" I ask, tucking a stray piece of hair behind her ear while my heart pounds like it wants out of my chest and into hers.

"That you'll leave." Her fingers twist in my shirt like she's afraid if she lets go I'll disappear. "That this is too good to be real. Everyone leaves eventually. My mom. My dad. Kasen— eventually he came back, but...still. Every guy I've let close enough to see the real me. I don't know if I could survive it if you—"

"I'm not going anywhere," I cut her off, the words coming out fiercer than I planned. "Not now, not ever. You're stuck with me, Freckles. For good."

She stares up at me, that war raging behind her eyes—she wants to believe me but she's scared shitless. Her hope is fighting with her fear. What she wants is battling her doubt. I hate that she's even got a fraction of a reason not to trust in us.

"How can you be so sure?" she whispers. "We've only been together a few months since we—"

Fuck, she's finally admitting we're together. About damn time.

"It's been years for me," I tell her, needing her to understand. "Years of wanting you. Years of loving you from a distance because I was convinced you'd never want me back. The second you let me in—let me touch you, hold you, love you—that was it for me. Game over. There is no going back. There's no life for me without you."

The silence stretches between us, and for a second I think maybe she's about to say she loves me too. Then my phone chirps with that specific tone I can't ignore. The emergency alert. I pull it from my pocket, already knowing whatever's on the screen is about to ruin everything.

"Banks?" Clover's voice comes out small and unsure, snapping me back to the moment.

"There's a fire." My blood turns to ice water in my veins when I recognize the address. My stomach plummets straight through the floor as images flash through my mind—Clover watching the news, Clover not knowing if I'm okay, Clover alone if something happens to me. The taste of copper floods my mouth as I bite the inside of my cheek hard enough to draw blood. I turn the screen so she can see it. "On Timber's block. They're calling everyone in."

I want to tell her not to worry, but if it's bad enough for an all-hands call and evacuating the whole block, we should absolutely be worried.

Her face pales. She doesn't ask if I'm going—she knows I have to. "Go." There's this resignation in her voice that kills me —like she's already preparing for the worst. For me to not come back to her. "Just...please be careful."

"Always." I press my forehead against hers, breathing her in for one more second. "This conversation isn't over, Freckles. Not even close."

I dig in my pocket and press the house key into her palm, folding her fingers around it. I hold on tight. "Whether you decide you want this place or not, this is yours. So you know you've always got somewhere to call home."

She stares at the key but I can't read her expression. She still hasn't said whether she wants to live here with me, to create a life together, to raise our baby.

She still hasn't said that she loves me back. But I can't wait around for answers.

"I gotta go," I tell her, already heading for the stairs. "I'll call you as soon as I can."

"Banks." Her voice brings me up short at the landing. I glance back, see her standing in what should be our bedroom, one hand on the bump that holds our future, the other clutching the key I gave her. "You better come home."

I manage a rough nod, then sprint out to my truck. As I peel away, her words echo in my mind—*everyone leaves eventually*. She's expecting me to vanish, to break her heart like every other person in her life.

I'm going to prove her wrong.

But first, I've got a fire to put out.

21
Clover

I HATE NEWS ANCHORS.

They all have the same plastic doom-and-gloom expression while they talk about "breaking news" with that weird mix of fake concern and barely contained glee. Like they're devastated about the four-alarm fire consuming an entire city block but also so fucking excited to be the one telling you about it.

"We're continuing our live coverage of the massive blaze that has engulfed several buildings in the industrial district," says the blonde woman on my TV, her helmet of hair not moving an inch as she gestures dramatically behind her. "As you can see, firefighters from multiple stations across Portland have responded to this dangerous situation."

The camera pans to show the inferno that used to be the block where my brother's brewery stands. Where Banks is right now, running toward danger while everyone else runs away. Fire licks up the sides of buildings, belching thick black smoke into the Portland sky. It's like watching the gates of hell open up in the middle of our city.

I chew on my nails and pace in front of the TV while my worst nightmare comes to life behind her.

"According to officials, the fire started in the Mexican restaurant adjacent to the popular local brewery, Timber, but quickly spread to neighboring businesses." The reporter's voice fades into background noise as I pace another circuit around my—our—apartment, my phone clutched in my hand.

It's been two hours since I caught a rideshare home after Banks left me standing in that beautiful house he bought without telling me, with a key pressed into my palm and those three words still hanging in the air between us.

I love you.

Three simple words that have me wanting to throw up for reasons that have nothing to do with pregnancy hormones. And now he's running into a burning building—because that's just what he does—and I'm left here with those words echoing in my head.

Why didn't I say them back?

I press redial for the eighth time, my heart sinking when Kasen's phone goes straight to voicemail again.

"It's me. Again. Call me back when you get this, okay? I need to know you're safe." I pause, my voice breaking as I try to contain the tsunami of sobs and snot and tears that are trying to break free. "Please."

I hang up and resume pacing, counting each step to keep from completely losing my mind. One Mississippi, two Mississippi, three Mississippi... Maybe if I count high enough, he'll call back. Maybe if I make it to a thousand, both Kasen and Banks will walk through the door safe.

The news anchor's voice breaks through my counting. "Officials are now confirming that all businesses on the block have been evacuated, but there are concerns that the fire could spread to additional buildings. The danger for first responders remains extremely high."

Extremely high. The words make my stomach twist and my

knees go shaky. I press my hand against my belly where our baby is growing. It's just the tiniest bump, enough that I can't button my jeans anymore and it looks like I had a huge burrito for lunch but not enough to really look pregnant yet. But there's a little piece of Banks in there and I just want him to be able to watch it grow.

"Your daddy's an idiot," I whisper to my belly. "Running into fires when he should be here with us."

But even as I say it, I know it's not true. It's who Banks is—the man who runs toward danger to help others. The man who can't stand by when someone needs him because his heart's so big. It's one of the thousands of things I love about him, even if it makes me want to strangle him sometimes.

Like now. Right now I could go for a good strangling.

After I know he's safe, obviously.

I check my phone again. Like I'd miss it going off with the volume all the way up and the vibration turned on, too. But still.

There's nothing.

There's a sharp knock at my door and I nearly jump out of my skin. I trip over my own feet because they won't move fast enough as I rush to answer it. The amount of hope that swells up inside of me is crazy, just this volcanic eruption of *please please please* that's overwhelming that it's Banks. Or my brother.

Fuck, I could lose them both. The only family I have left gone in a literal puff of smoke.

But when I yank the door open, it's Navy standing there with two hot drinks and a grim expression.

"Thought you might need company," she says, pushing past me into the apartment as all that hope leaks out of me and I do my best to not collapse to the floor in a pile of devastation. "And tea. Because you can't drink the good stuff and I'm drinking this in solidarity." She holds up her cup with a wrinkle of her nose.

"I've been calling Kasen for hours," I tell her, accepting the tea with shaking hands as I close the door. "He's not answering. What if he was at the brewery? What if he's hurt and no one's telling me? And Banks—" My voice breaks on his name, something that would mortify me if I wasn't freaking the fuck out.

Navy's arms are around me before I can finish the sentence, pulling me into a hug that smells like her favorite perfume and feels all kinds of wrong and right at the same time. As much as I love my bestie, hers aren't the arms I want to be in right now.

"Breathe," she orders, her voice gentle but firm. "Both those men are too stubborn to die in something as ordinary as a fire. Trust me."

I want to laugh, but it comes out wet, more like a sob.

"Come on," she says, guiding me to the couch. "Let's watch this disaster porn together, and you can tell me why you didn't text me back this morning."

My fingers tighten around the cup of tea. "Banks bought a house."

Navy's eyebrows shoot up toward her hairline. "He what now?"

"A house. In Sellwood. This gorgeous Craftsman with a big porch and four bedrooms and a kitchen that looks like it was created straight off my dream Pinterest board." The words tumble out in a rush. "He bought it without telling me, Navy. Just signed the papers and got the keys and then handed them to me like the grand gesture at the end of every romantic story ever."

"Was it?"

"Was it what?"

"Romantic," she clarifies, watching me with those too-perceptive eyes of hers. She knows how much I need to control everything. "Because from where I'm sitting, Mr. Ridiculously Hot Firefighter buying a house for you and your baby falls firmly into the category of 'romantic as fuck.'"

"He didn't just buy a house," I say, setting down my tea because my hands are shaking too much to hold it. "He told me he loves me. That he's been falling for me for years. That it's not about the baby or obligation or anything else. Just... me."

"And this is bad because...?"

"Because what if he's wrong?" The fear that's been choking me since Banks wrapped his hands around my face and told me he wants forever comes spilling out. "What if he thinks he loves me now, but in a year, or five years, or ten, he realizes it was just the excitement of the baby? Or he gets bored with my need to control everything? Or—"

"Or he gets killed in a fire and you never get the chance to tell him you love him too?" Navy cuts me off, her voice sharper than I've ever heard it. "Because that's what you're really afraid of, isn't it? Not that he'll leave. That he'll be taken from you."

Her words are like a knife slicing through me, spilling all my fears straight onto the floor. My mouth opens, but nothing comes out.

"You love that man," Navy continues, softer now. "I've watched you fall for him over these past months. Hell, I watched you pretend you hated him for years when it was so obvious you were obsessed with him just like he was obsessed with you. But you're so terrified of losing someone else you love that you'd rather push him away first."

"That's not—"

"It is," she insists. "And I get it. After your mom, I understand why you don't trust happiness to stick around. Then your dad couldn't cope, and he left, too. But Clover, this is Banks we're talking about. The man holds your hair back when you puke. He shows up every single time you need him, and even when you insist you don't. He was willing to give Kasen up for you."

My phone chimes with an incoming text, and I practically

dislocate my shoulder lifting it to my face to read it. It's from my brother and I let out a sob.

Kasen: Just heard from the fire captain that Banks is helping with the Timber block fire. He's not answering my calls. Have you heard anything from him?

Relief floods through me so intensely I actually feel lightheaded.

"Kasen's okay," I tell Navy, quickly texting back.

Navy squeezes my hand. "See? One down, one to go."

Me: No, nothing. And where the fuck have you been? I've called you like ten times, asshole.

Kasen: Shit, sorry

Kasen: It's been chaotic down here

Kasen: Talk later, but lmk if you hear from Banks

Me: Fine

Me: Stay safe

Me: If you die, I'll kill you

Kasen: Love you too

I toss my phone aside and rub my eyes, exhaustion and fear creating a toxic cocktail in my system. The tea's gone cold, but I drink it anyway, needing something to do with my hands.

"He put a lightning bolt mobile over the baby's crib," I say after a long silence, my voice sounding weird and echoey to own ears. "In the nursery at the new house. Because of the storm."

Navy gives me a soft smile. "The night you finally did something about your mutual pining?"

I nod, my throat suddenly too tight to speak.

"That's some romantic shit right there," she says. "He's good for you, you know. Has been since day one, even when you were too stubborn to see it."

"I see it now," I whisper, and it's the most honest I've been with myself in months, maybe years. "I'm just afraid it's too late."

"It's not," Navy says with a confidence I wish I could bottle and drink. "He'll be back. And when he is, you need to tell him exactly how you feel. No more stupid walls. No more pretending you don't need anyone."

The news anchor's voice rises with renewed urgency, drawing our attention back to the TV. "We're getting reports that part of the structure has collapsed, possibly trapping firefighters inside. Emergency crews are working to—"

I stop breathing. Literally just... stop. Like my lungs have forgotten how to function. The room spins around me as images flash across the screen—a building crumbling in on itself, firefighters running toward the collapse, the chaos of emergency vehicles and flashing lights. A vise clamps around my chest, squeezing tighter with every second that passes without news of Banks. My vision tunnels until all I can see is the fire on the screen, consuming everything in its path, possibly including the man I love.

"He's okay," Navy says, but the confidence in her voice has wavered. "Banks is too smart to get caught in something like that."

But isn't that exactly what he does? Run into burning buildings? Risk his life to save others? Didn't he tell me about the building collapse that left him with nightmares, pinned under rubble for hours?

My stomach lurches, and for a horrifying moment, I think I might throw up right here on my living room rug. I press my hand against my mouth and force the nausea down, my eyes never leaving the TV screen.

"I can't lose him," I whisper, the admission torn from some part of me I've kept locked away but that key Banks handed me earlier apparently unlocked more than the front door of our house. "I can't."

"You won't," Navy says, but we both know she can't promise that. No one can.

The next several hours stretch into eternity. Navy makes more tea. I ignore it. She orders food. I can't eat it. We sit in silence, watching the news as the fire is finally, gradually, brought under control. But there's no word about Banks, no list of injured firefighters, nothing but the terrible waiting.

Until my door opens without a knock.

22
Clover

HE'S STANDING THERE, still in his uniform pants and a clean PFD t-shirt he must have changed into at the station when he ditched his gear, though his face is still streaked with soot and his hair wet with sweat. His eyes find mine, and the relief in them mirrors what must be on my face.

He didn't even stop to shower, just came straight home to me.

"Banks." His name escapes my lips in a breathless rush, like all the air I've been holding in my lungs for hours leaves all at once. My body moves on instinct, my feet carrying me across the room before my brain can catch up. The relief is so powerful it's almost painful, making my chest ache and my knees weak as I throw myself at him.

He catches me in those strong arms of his, lifting me off my feet. I bury my face in his neck, breathing in the smell of smoke and sweat and that underlying scent that's just him, and I don't care that he's filthy or that I'm getting soot and ash all over my clothes.

He's alive. He's here. He came back to me.

To *us*.

"I'm okay," he murmurs against my hair, his voice rough like he's been breathing smoke for hours. Which he sort of has. "I'm sorry I couldn't call. It all happened so fast."

"Why'd you have to go?" I pull back just enough to see his face, my hands framing his jaw like he did to me at the house. My palms rub against his stubble. "You weren't even on shift. You could have stayed away. Been safe."

Something shifts in his expression—a hardness that appears for just a second before softening again. "They called for all available personnel. I couldn't just sit it out, Freckles. They needed help."

"You could have died." My voice breaks, all the fear of the past hours hitting me at once with enough force my legs actually buckle. His grip on me only tightens. "There was a collapse. They said on the news—"

"That was the back of the Mexican restaurant," he explains, his thumbs brushing over my cheekbones. "I was in the front, helping with the search."

I'm suddenly aware that Navy has slipped out without a word, leaving us alone. Part of me wants to be mad at her for abandoning me, but most of me is grateful for the privacy.

"You scared the hell out of me," I whisper, pressing my forehead against his chest. "Kasen wasn't answering his phone. I didn't know if either of you were okay."

"Kasen's fine. I checked on him first before coming here. I knew you'd be worried about him." His hand slides up to cradle the back of my neck. "He wasn't at the brewery when it started."

"I know. He finally texted me back." I pull away and wipe at my face, embarrassed to realize I'm crying. Again. These stupid pregnancy hormones are ruining my reputation. I wrinkle my nose. "You need a shower. You smell like a bonfire."

Banks laughs, the sound raspy but real, and relief washes through me all over again. "Trying to get me naked, Freckles?"

"Yes," I admit, surprising myself with my honesty. I think I surprise him too by the way his eyes he stares down at me. "I've been thinking about what you said. At the house."

His whole body goes still, those hazel eyes of his suddenly so intense I almost can't look at them directly. Like staring into the sun.

"Tell me."

I take a deep breath, searching for the words that have been forming in my heart for the past hours—hell, if I'm being honest, the past months.

Years.

"I've spent my whole life being afraid of needing anyone," I start slowly, the words feeling strange in my mouth. "After my mom died and my dad left, it just seemed safer to rely only on myself. To never give anyone else the power to devastate me like that again."

His dirty fingers come up to brush a strand of hair from my face, so gently I might cry again. "I know."

"I thought being alone meant being safe," I continue, forcing myself to hold his gaze even though every instinct is screaming at me to look away, to protect myself. "But watching that fire on the news today, not knowing if you were okay... I realized being without you is the most dangerous thing I could do to my heart."

His intake of breath is sharp. "Clover—"

"Let me finish," I interrupt, pressing my palms against his chest. His heart's racing in there, but I need to get this out before I lose my nerve. "God, I had this whole speech prepared in my head while I was watching that fire on TV, thinking you might be dead. And now I can't remember a single word of it."

I take a deep breath, my eyes locked on my hands against his chest rather than meeting his gaze.

"The thing is, I've spent my entire life organizing everything into neat little boxes with pretty color-coded labels. But you... you don't fit in any box. You're this hurricane that blew through my life, rearranged everything, and somehow made it all better."

I finally force myself to look up, meeting those hazel eyes that see right down to my soul.

"I hate that you made me need you." A laugh bubbles up, nervous and a little hysterical. "But I do. I can't do this life without you. And I love you and it terrifies me. Because loving you means accepting that you're always going to run toward fires. That you're always going to need to help people even if that means risking yourself. That I might lose you." My voice cracks, but I push through it, digging my fingers into his shirt.

"But I've spent the last four hours watching that fire on TV, imagining life without you, and I realized something. Not loving you would be worse. Not having you in my life would be worse than any risk."

His eyes are shining in a way I've never seen before, and it makes my throat tight so it's hard to get words out.

"And the house..." I laugh, and it's a little wet. The tears are starting to get in on the action now. "That ridiculous, beautiful house that you bought without consulting me or showing me a single listing, which is so completely not how normal people do things."

"Since when have we ever done anything the normal way?" he asks, a crooked grin tugging at his lips.

"Fair point." I take one of his hands, pressing it against my stomach where our baby is growing. "I love the house, Banks. I love the nursery and the kitchen and that stupid spice rack you installed even though it makes no sense to you. I love that you considered my plants. I love that you made a space that's just for me. I love that you thought about all the things I need before I even knew I needed them."

I look up as his arms slide back around my back like he can't stand any space between us. "But most of all, I love you. The firefighter who can't stop rescuing people, the man who learned how to make my grandmother's banana bread recipe when I mentioned missing it, the guy who puts my favorite mug under the coffee maker before he leaves for his shift so it's ready for me, and the one who somehow memorized every single place I'm ticklish just to make me laugh when I'm spiraling. Every stubborn, overprotective, ridiculously perfect inch of you."

"So does this mean you'll move in with me?" His voice is rough and I shiver. "Make that house our home?"

"Yes," I whisper, and the smile that breaks across his face is so beautiful it makes my chest ache. "But I have conditions."

I am still me, after all.

He laughs, his face lighting up with the same unbridled joy that only he can make me feel down to my bones. It makes him look about five years younger. "I would expect nothing less from you, Freckles. Hit me with your list."

"One," I hold up a finger, "you have to promise not to die in a fire. I mean it. You stay safe out there, or I'll kill you myself."

Banks's grin turns into something more serious. "I'm always careful. You and this baby are my whole world now." He doesn't promise because we both know he can't, so I let it go.

"Two," I continue, trying to ignore how his words make my heart do somersaults, "I want to paint the master bedroom. That beige is depressing."

"Whatever color you want," he agrees immediately. "Even if it's that weird purple you have in your linen closet here."

I wave him off. "That was here when I moved in and it's ugly as hell. And three," I say, my voice suddenly shy, "I want you to fuck me right now and show me exactly how much you love me. Because I've been watching the news for four hours thinking you might be dead, and I really need to feel you alive inside of me."

His eyes darken, and the look on his face makes me squirm because that look right there? It promises very dirty things.

"That," he says, his voice dropping to that gravelly register that turns me to liquid, "I can definitely do."

He's filthy from the fire, but I don't care. His mouth tastes like smoke and salt when he crushes his lips to mine, his arms banding around my waist and lifting me off my feet. I wrap my legs around his hips, gasping when I feel how hard he already is beneath his black uniform pants.

"I love you," he growls against my mouth as he carries me toward the bedroom. "Fuck, I love you so much it scares me sometimes."

"I love you too," I whisper, and the words come easier this time. Less terrifying. "Now get these disgusting clothes off and get in the shower before I change my mind."

His laugh rumbles through his chest and into mine. "Bossy as ever."

"You love it."

"I love you," he corrects, setting me down on the bathroom counter. "The bossiness is just a bonus."

His pants hit the floor followed by his t-shirt. I drink in the sight of him—that ridiculous body that makes my mouth water, the tattoos rippling over muscle as he moves, the exhaustion evident in the set of his shoulders.

He turns on the shower and holds out his hand to me. "Join me?"

Ten minutes later, we're both clean, my back pressed against the tile wall of the shower as Banks kneels in front of me, his mouth between my thighs, forcing me to feel nothing but him. His hands grip my hips, keeping me upright when my knees threaten to buckle, and the hot water runs over us both as he works me with his tongue until I'm gasping his name.

"Missed this," he groans against my pussy, the vibration making me shudder. "Missed the way you taste. The sounds you make when you come for me."

"You were only gone a few hours." *A few hours that took ten years off my life.*

"Don't care," he says between licks. "It was too long."

I gasp when he hits a sensitive spot, my fingers tangling in his wet hair. "I need you inside me. Now."

He's on his feet so fast he slips a little and I laugh, but then it dies when he spins me around so I'm facing the wall, his front pressed to my back. My face presses against the cold tile as one of his big, calloused hands slides around to cup my breast, his thumb brushing over my nipple.

"Like this?" he asks, his breath hot against my ear. "You want my big dick in your tight little pussy, Freckles? Want me to take what I want?"

I whimper when I feel the thick, heavy length of him rub against my ass, his fingers pinching my nipple. "Yes, please, yes."

His other hand slides up my thigh, yanking my legs apart while he pushes me further against the wall so I bend. The head of his cock slides against me, slick with pre-cum that mixes with my arousal. He's right where I want him, where I *need* him, and when he thrusts, it's with enough force to make my body slide up the tile. He does it again and again, fucking me with a force that makes the head of his cock hit places inside of me that make me weak.

My palms flatten against the tile, bracing myself as he sets a rhythm that's just on the right side of rough.

"Mine," he growls, his voice a rumble I feel all the way down my spine. "Say it, Clover. Tell me you're mine."

"Yours," I gasp as he hits places inside me that curl my toes. "I'm yours."

His hand slides down to rub against my clit, and I nearly burst out of my skin at the rightness of it. It's so good. So, *so* good. "And I'm yours," he says, his voice suddenly soft and reverent even as his body pounds into mine. "Only ever yours, Freckles."

The intensity of it all—his words, his touch, the emotional rollercoaster of the day—sends me over the edge embarrassingly fast. I come with his name on my lips, my body clenching around him as wave after wave of pleasure crashes through me.

He follows seconds later, his forehead pressing against my shoulder as he pulses inside me, my name a broken sound on his lips.

For a long moment, we just stand there under the cooling water, his arms wrapped around me from behind, his hands splayed protectively over my stomach where our baby grows.

"We should probably get out before we freeze," I finally say, hating that I have to move away from him at all but the water's starting to get uncomfortable.

Banks presses a kiss to my shoulder. "Probably. But I'm not ready to let you go just yet."

"You don't have to," I tell him, turning in his arms to face him. "Not ever again."

The smile he gives me is soft and sweet, so different from his usual cocky grin that it makes my chest ache. "Promise?"

"Promise." I stand on my tiptoes to press a gentle kiss to his lips. "Now get me to bed before I fall asleep standing up. Today has been... a lot."

He laughs and reaches behind me to turn off the water. "Has it really only been one day? Feels like a lifetime since I showed you the house."

"A good lifetime or a bad one?" I ask, suddenly uncertain.

Banks wraps a towel around me, his movements careful and tender. "The best, Freckles. Absolutely the best."

Later—much later—we lie together in my bed, his hand resting over my belly. He looks wrecked with purple smudges under his eyes that I can see even in the darkness.

"Sleep," I tell him, brushing my fingers through his hair. "You've had a long day."

"Don't want to close my eyes," he murmurs, already half-gone. "Might wake up and find out this was all a dream."

"It's not a dream," I whisper, pressing a kiss to his forehead. "I'll be right here when you wake up. Promise."

His arm tightens around me. "Love you."

"Love you too."

And as Banks's breathing evens out into sleep, his hand still protectively settled over the place where our baby grows, I realize something important. For the first time in my life, I'm not counting down the days until something ends. Not viewing this as temporary or conditional or something that will inevitably be taken from me.

For the first time, I'm letting myself believe in forever.

And it feels like coming home.

23
Banks

THE LAST TWO months have flown by since the fire that nearly destroyed my best friend's brewery. I'm still having nightmares about finding Clover alone in our house, clutching her stomach while she tells me I didn't make it back. But one look at her now—her black hair piled on top of her head in a messy bun, wearing a dress that shows off her six-month belly, laughing at something Navy said—is enough to make my heart settle back into its normal rhythm.

Christ, I love her.

Kasen really went all out for Timber's grand reopening. The place looks better than before the fire—new tables, new taps, but he managed to salvage the original bar top that his grandfather installed way back when. The whole place is packed with locals, regulars, and firefighters from my station celebrating both the brewery's resurrection and the fact Kasen didn't murder me once he found out I knocked up his sister.

I watch Clover weave through the crowd—stopping to talk to the firefighters from my station, laughing with Theo, checking on the buffet table like she isn't six months pregnant and supposed to take it easy. Thank fuck her hyperemesis finally eased up, because now she's rocking the pregnancy glow everyone raves about. Or maybe that's just how she looks to me now that she's carrying my kid and wearing my ring.

Yeah, we've had a busy couple of months.

"You're staring again," Reed says, appearing beside me with a beer in his hand. It's still weird sometimes to think of him as Reed instead of Dr. Walker, but it's hard to stay formal with a guy who's as big of a die-hard Blazers fan as you are. The dude knows more obscure basketball stats than anyone I've ever met. "Though I'd probably stare too if it were my kid in there."

Amazing how the same doc I wanted to deck for touching Clover ended up a close friend. Sports, man.

"Can't help it," I admit, taking a swig of my own beer. "I still can't believe she said yes."

"To which part?" Reed grins. "The baby, the house, or the ring?"

"All of the above." I shake my head. "I keep waiting for her to realize she could do better."

He snorts. "Highly doubtful. You two are so in love it's uncomfortable to witness." Then he hits me with that smug doctor look that makes me want to launch a bar stool at him. "Still dying to know what I've known for a week? Your begging's hit peak embarrassment levels."

"Come on, man." I lower my voice, leaning in. "Just tell me. Doctor-patient confidentiality doesn't count with the father."

"Yeah, it does," he counters, smirk widening. "And Clover would literally murder me if I ruin Kasen's moment."

"I won't breathe a word," I insist. "Not even to her."

Reed taps his watch. "Nice try. Kasen'll be making the announcement any minute. You can wait like everyone else."

After last week's sonogram, Clover decided her brother should be the one to announce the baby's sex—partly because she thinks it's hilarious to make him wait, and partly to make up for the fact that Navy knew about the pregnancy weeks before he did. I've been bugging Reed nonstop, but the bastard's a steel trap.

"Fine," I mutter, scanning the room for my future brother-in-law. "He's been guarding that envelope like it's got the nuclear launch codes inside."

But it's not Kasen I spot. It's the woman who just walked in. She's tall, with pink waves of hair and a smile on her face that only slightly hides her shark-like nature. As soon as I spot her, I start looking harder for my best friend.

"Who's that?" Reed asks, following my gaze.

"Trouble," I say, watching Navy rush over to hug her. "That's Wren. She runs Cascade Craft Distribution."

"Ah." Reed's chin lifts. "The competition."

"Not just competition," I correct. "From what Kasen's said, she's been trying to poach Timber's accounts for the past year. She undercut his prices by three percent last quarter and stole the airport concession contract they've had for years."

"And Navy invited her to his reopening?" He looks incredulous. "That's cold."

"I'm guessing Navy doesn't know about their business beef," I say, already scanning the room for Kasen. I spot him behind the bar, mid-laugh at something Brenna's saying. Then his gaze shifts to the door. The second he sees Wren, he goes rigid—smile wiped off his face and replaced by a scowl.

"This might get entertaining," Reed says.

Reed and I watch as Kasen says something to Brenna and makes his way out from behind the bar, intercepting Navy and Wren before they get too far into the crowd.

"She looks just as irritated as he does."

"Twenty bucks says he tells her to get out," I say.

"How stupid do you think I am?" Reed asks. "Of course he'll tell her to get out." Reed takes a sip of his beer. "But is it just me or is he," he squints at Kase, "eye fucking her a little?"

"Thank you!" I throw my hand out in their direction.

"Finally someone else sees that shit. It's like he can't decide if he wants to strangle her or—"

"Tap more than the beer," Reed finishes with a laugh and I clink my beer with his.

Across the room, I catch Clover's eye. She tilts her head in that questioning way she does when she senses something's off, and I give her a small nod toward Kasen and Wren. Her eyebrows shoot up in recognition, then she beelines for us.

"Incoming," Reed warns, straightening up a bit. He's still a little formal around Clover sometimes, like he can't quite shed the doctor-patient dynamic.

"What's going on with my brother?" she asks as soon as she reaches us, looping her arm through mine and laying her head on my shoulder. "He looks like he's about to have an aneurysm."

"Navy brought a surprise guest," I explain, dropping a kiss on the top of her head. "That's Wren. The woman behind Cascade."

"Ugh," Clover groans. "Kasen has done nothing but bitch about this woman for months. What's Navy thinking? This is going to be a disaster."

"Or highly entertaining," I counter. "Depends on how you look at it."

She rolls her eyes, but a smile quirks her lips. "Behave, Priestly. This is his night."

I give her my best innocent look. "I'm always on my best behavior."

"Mmhmm," Clover says, turning toward Reed with a wry smile. "Has he been watching my brother's meltdown like it's primetime TV for long?"

"Only about five minutes," Reed answers, flashing a quick grin. "But honestly, can you blame him? It's the most excitement we've had all night."

Clover sighs, leaning against me so I can feel the gentle pressure of her stomach at my side. "I should probably go rescue Navy from that mess before Kasen says something he's gonna regret."

"Let her handle it," I say, slipping an arm around Clover's waist. "She's a grown woman. And aren't you supposed to be taking it easy? Doctor's orders, right?" I shoot a pointed look at Reed, who raises his hands in a defensive shrug.

"Hey, don't look at me," he says. "I already told her to not push herself. It's up to you to make sure she listens."

Clover narrows her eyes at both of us. "I see how it is—now you two team up against me."

"Only because we care," Reed says, and I'm struck again by how quickly he's become part of our circle. "And because your fiancé would probably set my car on fire if I didn't remind you."

"I would never," I protest. "Too easy to trace."

That gets a genuine laugh from both of them, and I feel a surge of pride at the sound. Making Clover laugh is still my favorite accomplishment.

The tension across the room seems to have eased a bit. No one's shouting or throwing punches, so I'll call that a win.

"So," Reed says after a beat, a thoughtful look on his face, "I've been trying to calculate the statistical odds your baby inherits Clover's eye color based on the genetic markers I observed in her medical workup and well"—he gestures at my face—"your apparent phenotypes."

Clover and I just stare at him.

"What?" he asks, seeming genuinely confused by our reaction.

"Dude," I say, barely holding back a laugh, "normal people fill the silence with sports or the weather, not whatever that was."

Reed's cheeks flush as he scowls. "Well, I hate small talk." He takes a large gulp of his beer. "Sue me."

Sometimes Reed says the most random shit and I can tell it embarrasses him, but he doesn't really get the whole being social thing. He's awkward as hell, but it's part of his charm. You can't help but like the guy—he's somehow both brilliant and completely clueless at the same time.

I'm still laughing when Kasen joins us, his expression all the way annoyed.

"Enjoying yourselves?" he asks dryly.

"More than you, apparently," I shoot back. "How's the chat with your new best friend?"

He shoots me a look that would wither most men. "She's not my friend."

"Business rival, then," I shrug, enjoying this way too much. "Or is 'arch-nemesis' more accurate?"

"The bane of his existence," Clover adds with a mischievous smile that I adore. God, I love this woman.

"Very funny." Kasen takes a long pull from his beer. "Navy had no idea about the airport contract. Or any of it. Wren's been feeding her some bullshit no doubt."

"And you set her straight?" Reed asks.

"Tried to. Navy thinks I'm overreacting." Kasen scrubs a hand through his hair, frustration etched on his face. "Swears Wren's just doing her job."

"Is she wrong, though?" Clover asks gently.

Kasen's eyes narrow. "Whose side are you on?"

"Yours, obviously," she says, unfazed. "I'm just saying it's business, Kase. She's not exactly breaking any laws."

"It feels personal," he insists. "Targeting that airport contract in particular—she knew how important that was to Timber."

"Maybe it *is* personal," I suggest. "Maybe she hates you for some reason. What'd you do?"

"Nothing," he snaps. "We've only met a couple of time and she's always been the fucking worst."

Clover and I exchange a look, but before either of us can push further, Navy bounces over, eyes shining.

"It's time!" she announces. "Everyone's ready for the reveal."

Immediately, Kasen's entire demeanor shifts; he brightens like someone flipped a switch. He taps the pocket with that infamous envelope. "Finally. I've been dying to open this thing."

We trail after him toward the center of the brewery, where he hops onto a chair and whistles to stop the chatter.

"First, a big thanks for coming out tonight," he begins, voice carrying over the quieting crowd "Rebuilding after the fire wasn't easy, but seeing all of you here makes it worth every minute of the past two months."

The place erupts in cheers and raised glasses.

"And now," Kasen continues, "I have the honor of sharing some news that's even better than Timber reopening. As most of you know, my sister and her fiancé are expecting their first child."

Another wave of whoops and catcalls—this time from my fellow firefighters in the corner.

"What you don't know is that I'm holding the envelope revealing whether I'm getting a niece or nephew." He waves the sealed envelope overhead. "And since I found out about the pregnancy after half of Portland already did,"—he levels a playful glare at Navy, who shrugs innocently—" they gave me the honor of sharing the news."

Clover leans back against my chest, and I wrap my arms around her, my hands resting on her belly where the baby pushes against my palm. In this moment—surrounded by friends, holding the woman I love while she carries our child—I feel a completeness I never knew was possible.

Kasen rips open the envelope with an overly dramatic flourish, pulls out the card, scans it—and a huge grin lights his face.

"Ladies and gentlemen," he proclaims, "I am thrilled to announce that the newest addition to our family will be…"

He pauses, just to fuck with us.

"A boy! I'm getting a nephew!"

The room explodes into cheers, and I tighten my arms around Clover, pressing a kiss to the top of her head. A son. We're having a son.

"Told you," she murmurs, turning her face up to mine. "Mother's intuition."

"Should've listened to you, Freckles." I brush my lips over her forehead, choking back the weirdly intense surge of emotion welling up in my chest. A son. A little boy, maybe with Clover's blue eyes and that same iron will, or maybe he'll get my height and a tendency to take everything apart just to see how it works. "But the next one's definitely gonna be a girl."

Her eyes narrow. "Next one?"

I pretend not to hear her as the party kicks into an even higher gear. Morgan hands out cigars to the station crew, Theo toasts with a fresh round of drinks, and Navy ties blue ribbons onto anything that isn't moving.

I lose track of Clover for a bit—she's drifting through the crowd, fielding a barrage of name questions and letting everyone congratulate her. We've batted around Noble Jensen—she says Noble because that's how she sees me and Jensen after my dad—but I'm not pushing. There's plenty of time to decide.

I'm grabbing a beer when Reed appears at my side again, this time towing Kasen behind him.

"So," Kasen starts, "is it weird for you that Reed's seen Clover's... you know." He waves a hand vaguely southward.

Reed groans. "Are we still on this?"

"It's a legit question," Kasen insists. "I'd be freaked if one of my buddies had seen my girlfriend's... lady parts."

"Lady parts?" I echo, almost choking on my beer. "What are you, twelve?"

"You know what I mean."

Reed sighs. "I'm a doctor. I've seen thousands of—" He

cringes, "—*lady parts*, if that's how we're phrasing it now. It's clinical."

"Sure, but now you're tossing back beers with the husband of said lady parts," Kasen points out. "That's different."

"Fiancé," I correct. "And would you stop saying 'lady parts'? Jesus. She's your sister."

He shrugs. "Yeah, well, I'm trying not to think about it that hard. But fine. *Vagina*. Is that better?" Kasen's definitely had one too many, because now he's trying to stir shit up.

"Can we please talk about literally anything else?" Reed glances skyward like he's praying for lightning to strike him. "I'd rather discuss the biochemical process of how your IPA ferments than this."

"I'm with Reed," I say. "But to answer your question—no, it's not weird. He's a doctor, it's his job."

"Thank you," Reed mutters, relieved.

"Although," I add, smirking, "if he starts drooling whenever Clover walks by, we'll have problems."

Reed punches me in the arm. "You're an asshole."

"Guilty."

Kasen shakes his head, laughing, and the two of them start talking about the Ducks' upcoming season. I tune them out when I spot Clover across the room, one hand resting on her belly as she chats with Brenna. As if sensing my gaze, she looks up and gives me that smile—the one that's just for me, that crinkles the corners of her eyes and makes my heart do backflips like I'm a fucking teenager with his first crush.

Eventually, Kasen peels off, meandering suspiciously close to where Wren's standing alone, studying his vintage tap display.

"Twenty bucks says he's talking to her again within five minutes," Reed says, following my gaze.

"You're on." I shake his hand. "He'll hold out for ten. Clover's stubbornness runs in the family."

"Given how many times he's looked her way in the last two minutes, plus the amount of beer he's had? Bad bet." He glances at his watch with a smirk. "I don't need a medical degree needed to diagnose a serious case of 'can't-stay-away-from-her.'"

"You're such a nerd," I laugh, but keep an eye on Kasen's slow orbit around Wren. Then I slip away to join Clover, sliding an arm around her waist as she chats with Brenna.

I excuse myself from Reed and make my way to Clover, sliding an arm around her waist as I join her conversation with Brenna.

"Banks was just telling us how he knew it was a boy all along," Brenna says with a shit-eating grin.

"Oh, really?" Clover gives me a look of pure skepticism. "That's odd, because last week you were sure it was a girl."

"I was just preparing you for the possibility," I say smoothly. "Deep down, I always knew."

"Uh-huh." She doesn't believe me for a second, but her eyes are filled with all the love and tolerance for my bullshit in the world. "Whatever you say, Priestly."

"Ladies and gentlemen!" Navy's voice cracks through the noise like a whip. "If I could have your attention for one more second!"

We all turn to see her standing on a chair, mic in hand.

"What's she doing?" Clover whispers.

"No clue," I admit, just as lost.

"As you all know, we're celebrating two amazing things tonight," Navy continues. "The return of Timber, bigger and better than ever, and the news that baby Priestly is officially a boy!"

Cheers erupt around us again.

"But there's one more thing we should celebrate," she says, her eyes finding us in the crowd. "Banks and Clover, could you come up here, please?"

Clover looks up at me, confusion clear on her face. "Did you know about this?"

"Not a clue," I admit, guiding her toward Navy. "But you know how she gets when she has an idea."

We push toward the front, and Navy hops down from the chair, handing me the mic.

"You two want to tell everyone your other news?" she prompts.

Ah. That news.

I glance at Clover, silently asking permission. She gives me a small nod, her cheeks flushing that pretty pink I love so much.

"Well," I say into the mic, "since Navy's decided to put us on the spot..."

The crowd laughs, and I pull Clover closer to my side.

"Some of you know Clover and I are engaged," I begin. "And until this week, we were thinking we'd wait 'til after Noble arrives to tie the knot—"

Murmurs ripple through the crowd at the baby-name reveal, and Clover jabs me lightly in the ribs.

"Spoiler alert," I add with a grin, earning more laughter. "But we changed our minds. So three weeks from today, this amazing woman is going to make me the luckiest bastard in Portland by becoming my wife."

The cheers erupt again, and I pass the mic back to Navy, turning to Clover.

"Sorry," I murmur in her ear. "I had no idea she was gonna do that."

"It's okay," she says, surprising me. "Everyone was going to find out soon anyway."

I kiss her then, keeping it brief but loaded with everything I feel—love, gratitude, and the absolute conviction that she's the best thing that's ever happened to me.

When we break apart, the party surges back to life. Morgan

and Vetter are already scheming up a bachelor party that sounds like it'll end with needing bail money, and Navy and Brenna have Clover cornered—no doubt grilling her about wedding colors or who's getting invited. It's a crazy, perfect snapshot of our life right now.

I head to the bar for water—gotta keep my pregnant fiancée hydrated—and find Reed loitering there.

"Three weeks, huh?" he says, clapping my shoulder. "That's fast."

"Time's ticking, and Clover's belly isn't getting any smaller," I reply, shrugging. "We figure we might as well lock it down before she can't waddle down the aisle."

He laughs, raising his beer. "Congrats again, man. Seriously."

"Thanks." I glance across the room, where Clover is laughing at something Brenna said. "You'll be there, right?"

"Wouldn't miss it."

As the bartender hands me Clover's water, I notice movement by the kitchen door—Kasen and Wren, locked in what appears to be a heated conversation. She's gesturing animatedly while he stands with his arms crossed scowling at her.

"Your beer's not bad, James," I can just barely hear Wren saying. "But your distribution strategy is stuck in the last decade. Don't blame me for taking advantage."

"Not all of us need gimmicks to sell our product," Kasen fires back. "Some of us still believe in quality over flashy packaging."

Neither notices me watching until I clear my throat, and Wren immediately steps back, smoothing down her jeans as though that'll hide how tense she is.

"I should go," she says. "Congrats on the re-opening."

She gives me a tight smile and slips past us, leaving Kasen glaring after her.

I raise an eyebrow at him. "You want to explain what that was about?"

"You want to explain why I shouldn't punch you again for fucking my sister?" he asks, and I roll my eyes.

"How long are you gonna hold that against me?"

He just glares and drinks his beer instead of answering.

"Yeah, that's what I thought."

Clover joins us, wrapping an arm around my waist. "What's my brother looking so murder-y about?"

I hand her the water and pull her closer, my hand curving protectively over her belly. "We were just talking about how life throws the best curveballs when you least expect them."

"Speak for yourself," Kasen grumbles, but there's less heat in it now. His eyes drift to the door, where Wren is talking to Navy. "Some curveballs are just meant to strike you out."

"Says the man who swings at everything," Clover teases, bumping her shoulder against his. She's got no clue what we're talking about, but I have a feeling Kase's going to have his own reckoning soon.

The rest of the night is a blur of well-wishes, beer, and Navy's increasingly over-the-top wedding plans. Kasen's got his brewery back, Clover's glowing, and I've got my arm around my pregnant fiancée, who's carrying my son. Hard to beat that for a Friday night.

Later, I'm driving us home and Clover reaches over to grab my hand, her smaller fingers linking with mine.

"That wasn't half bad," she says with a tired smile. "Even with my brother acting like an idiot around Wren."

"Are you kidding? That was the best part," I say, giving her hand a squeeze. "Watching those two idiots orbit around each other all night. I bet they bang it out within a month.'"

She rolls her eyes but snickers. "You're such an ass."

"Yeah, but I'm your ass."

"True." She sighs. "I love you. Noble and I both do."

Damn if those three words don't still slam into with all the force of an earthquake every time.

I reach over and lay my free hand on her belly, feeling my son shift. Every time he moves around in there, it's like I turn into the Grinch and my heart grows three sizes. Nothing else hits like that feeling.

"Love you too, Freckles. Both of you."

We pull onto our street, the glow from the dash lighting her face, eyes half-shut with exhaustion, one hand resting over our son. Six months ago, I was sleeping on her tiny-ass futon, making coffee in her kitchen, pretending not to stare at her in those sleep shorts that drove me fucking wild. Back then, I thought we'd go our separate ways once my apartment was fixed. That we'd keep living in denial of how we felt about each other.

Now I know better. We were always heading here—to this baby, this house, this life. And in three weeks, I'm making her mine, officially and forever. Not bad for a guy who used to run from the word "commitment" like it was on fire.

It hits me like a lightning bolt—that perfect clarity that only comes a few times in life. I pull the truck into our driveway and kill the engine, but neither of us moves to get out.

"You know," I say, breaking the thick, comfortable quiet, "I think we were inevitable, you and me."

She cracks an eye open, mouth curving into a wicked little grin. "Inevitable? That's a big word for a firefighter."

"Smartass." I reach over to tuck a strand of hair behind her ear. "But yeah, inevitable. Like gravity or the tide or some shit. You can fight it all you want, but some forces in the universe will always win."

Clover rolls her eyes, but her expression is gentle. "So the universe conspired to push us together? That it?"

"I think," I say slowly, choosing my words carefully because I need her to understand this, "that from the first moment I saw you rolling your eyes at your brother across that party, there was never going to be another ending for me. Every choice, every road was always going to lead right back to you."

She's silent for a beat, and in the faint light, I catch the shimmer of tears. "That's either the most romantic thing I've ever heard or the biggest load of bullshit."

I chuckle, because that's my girl—refusing to be swept away even when I'm baring my soul. "Why not both? The universe shoved us together, and I bullshitted you into loving me."

She gives me her heart-stopping smile, the one that I'd do anything for. "The thing is, Banks," she says, her voice suddenly serious, "I think you might be right. No matter how hard I tried to fight it, somehow we were always meant to end up here. Together. Even when it made no sense."

I capture her hand and bring it to my lips. "Of course I'm right. You'll learn soon enough—I'm always right."

She tilts her head back and does the best thing in the world...

She laughs.

EPILOGUE
Banks

THREE MONTHS LATER...

"You are never, ever touching me again, you fucking asshole!"

Clover's grip on my hand tightens like a goddamn vise as another contraction hits her. Her face contorts, a sheen of sweat covering her forehead as she bears down, then collapses back against the hospital bed, panting.

"You're doing amazing, baby," I tell her, brushing damp strands of hair off her face. "You're the strongest person I've ever met."

"Don't sweet-talk me right now," she growls, but she refuses to let go of my hand. "This is your fault. You and your stupid dick. I hate you so much."

Reed coughs as he tries to hide his laugh, and I flip him off with my other hand.

I bite back my own grin because laughing right now would probably get me murdered. "I know, Freckles. You can hate me all you want as long as you keep pushing."

It's been eighteen hours since Clover's water broke in the middle of the night, and I got the call at the station that it was time. Eighteen hours of watching the woman I love fight through pain I can't even imagine. Eighteen hours of feeling completely fucking helpless and doing my best to be her rock at the same time.

At least Reed's here. Crazy how far we've come from me wanting to punch him at that first ultrasound. Now he's the guy who shows up with weird basketball stats and embarrasses himself after a few beers—but there's nobody I trust more with Clover and our baby.

Reed moves between Clover's legs, professional mode fully engaged. It's almost comforting how he morphs from our awkward friend to the confident doctor the second he steps into his role.

"You're at ten centimeters, Clover," he tells her with an encouraging nod. "Time to push with the next contraction. You ready to meet this baby?"

Clover nods, her grip on my hand tightening even more.

A flash of panic crosses her face as she looks up at me. For all her bravado, all her insistence that she can handle anything, I've never seen her look so scared.

"I've got you," I whisper, pressing my lips to her temple. "I'm not going anywhere."

Three months ago, we stood in front of our friends and family as Clover became my wife in a small ceremony in our backyard. She was seven months pregnant, glowing in a simple white dress that showed off her belly, and I thought nothing could ever make me feel more complete than that moment.

I was wrong.

Because now, as Clover grits her teeth and bears down with another contraction, cursing my existence with every curse word in her arsenal, I'm watching her bring our son into the world. And holy shit, there's nothing more badass than that.

"I can see the head," Reed says. "One more big push, Clover."

"You said that three pushes ago!" she snaps, but then

another contraction hits, and she crushes my hand with a force I didn't know was humanly possible.

"That's it," I tell her, trying to keep my voice steady. "Almost there, baby. You've got this."

A primal sound tears from her throat—half-scream, half-grunt—and then suddenly there's a new sound in the room. A tiny, angry cry that stops my heart mid-beat.

"It's a boy!" Reed announces with genuine excitement breaking through his usual doctor cool. He lifts our son up so we can see him, a tiny, red-faced, screaming miracle covered in God-knows-what and absolutely perfect.

My vision blurs, the world going watery as the ground shifts under my feet. I've run into burning buildings, felt the floor give way beneath me, seen death up close—but nothing—nothing—has ever rocked me like this. This tiny human Clover and I made, half her, half me, and somehow already his own person.

"He's here," I manage, voice wrecked. My hand shakes as I reach toward him but pull back, suddenly terrified of how breakable he looks. "Look what you did, Freckles. Look what we made."

"He's perfect," Clover whispers beside me, her voice raw with emotion and exhaustion. "Banks, look at him."

As if I could look anywhere else.

The tears I've been fighting spill over, streaming unchecked down my face. I don't bother wiping them away—can't even find the coordination to try. Every wall I've ever built crumbles at the sound of my son's cries.

"I know," I whisper, bending to press my forehead against Clover's, my tears mingling with hers. "You're incredible. I don't—I can't even—" My words fail completely, a sob breaking free from somewhere deep in my chest.

She reaches up with a shaking hand to touch my face, her eyes bright with tears and exhaustion but filled with a love so fierce it's almost blinding. "We did it," she whispers. "He's really here."

"I love you so much," I tell her, though it doesn't come close to what I'm feeling. "I always thought I was brave because I fight fires, but you—what you just did—that's real courage."

Reed personally brings our son over instead of having a nurse do it, carefully placing him in Clover's arms with a gentleness that reminds me why we trusted him with this in the first place. The awkward guy who once rattled off statistics at our engagement party is the same one who's now sharing one of the most important moments of our lives.

"He scores a nine on the Apgar," Reed says quietly, clearly proud. "It's an excellent score."

Clover looks down at Noble with such wonder that my chest physically aches. Then she looks up at me, tears tracking down her flushed cheeks.

"Want to hold your son?" she asks.

My hands tremble as I reach for him. I've held babies before —but never my own. Nothing prepares me for the feeling of holding my own child for the first time. The second his tiny body settles into the crook of my arm, the entire universe tilts. His face scrunches up as he squints against the bright lights of the delivery room.

"Hey, little man," I whisper, my voice breaking. "I'm your dad."

His eyes crack open at the sound of my voice, and even though I know newborns can't see clearly, it feels like he's looking right at me. This tiny person knows he's mine and I'm his.

"Noble Jensen Priestly," I say, testing his name out loud for the first time. It fits him—strong but not overbearing. A name he can grow into.

"I think he looks like you," Clover says, reaching out to touch his tiny hand. "Poor kid."

I let out a laugh, still unable to tear my gaze from him. "Nah, that chin's all you. And that little nose."

"Well those are definitely your ears. Plus, he's got the same hair color as you do."

We're both crying and grinning and staring at this miracle we created during a thunderstorm almost a year ago. I lean down to kiss Clover's damp forehead.

"I love you," I say, voice thick. "So goddamn much."

"I love you too," she whispers against my mouth. "Even if I did threaten to castrate you."

"Worth it," I say, glancing down at Noble. "Every threat, every broken bone in my hand, all of it. Worth it for him."

A week later, I'm pacing our new nursery at three in the morning, Noble tucked against my chest while I try to lull him back to sleep. Clover's finally crashed in our bed after taking the brunt of night feedings the day before, so I'm determined to give her a break.

"You gotta cut your mom some slack, bud," I murmur, moving in slow circles as he squirms against me. "She's tough, but she needs sleep too."

He makes a small snuffling sound but doesn't start screaming, his tiny body warm against mine. I still can't get over how perfect he is—ten fingers, ten toes, a little tuft of dark hair, and a set of lungs that lets the whole neighborhood know when he's hungry.

"Your mom is the strongest person I've ever met," I continue, keeping my voice low. "Smartest, too. And the most stubborn. Which means you and I are going to have our hands full." I brush my finger gently over his cheek. "But that's okay. We're going to protect her heart anyway. She spends so much time taking care of everyone else, but you and me? We're going to make sure she knows she's loved. Every single day."

Maybe it's the rumble of my voice or the slow swaying, but Noble settles, his tiny breath evening out. For a minute, I stand there in the glow of the nightlight, memorizing the weight of him in my arms, the smell of his head, soaking in the sensation of holding my son.

A floorboard creaks, and I glance up to see Clover standing in the doorway, watching us. She's wearing one of my old PFD t-shirts and those tiny sleep shorts that still always do me in, her hair piled on top of her head in that messy bun. Even with shadows under her eyes and spit-up on her shoulder, she's the most beautiful thing I've ever seen.

"Hey," I whisper. "Did we wake you?"

She shakes her head, moving into the nursery. "No. The empty bed did." She comes to stand beside us, reaching out to brush her fingers over Noble's back. "How long has he been out?"

"About twenty minutes. I thought I'd give him a little more time before putting him down to be sure he was fully under."

She smiles at me, and it hits me all over again—how fucking lucky I am that this incredible woman chose me. Chose this life with me.

"Let me take him," she says. "You've been on your feet since your shift ended, and you have to be back at the station in six hours."

I want to argue, to tell her I'm fine, that she needs rest more than I do. But I'm learning that sometimes the best way to take care of Clover is to let her take care of me.

"Thanks, Freckles," I say, handing him over. She takes our son like she's done this forever, and it still amazes me, considering we've only been doing this for a week.

"Go get some sleep," she says, settling into the rocking chair in the corner of the nursery. "I've got him."

I lean down to press a kiss to the top of her head, then Noble's. "Wake me if you need anything. Promise?"

"Promise," she says with a small smile. " By the way, there's some stuff on the kitchen table I want you to look at tomorrow. Bar logo ideas. They're super rough, but I think I'm onto something."

"Can't wait." I tell her, already looking forward to it. She's been dreaming of running her own bar for years, and I'm lucky enough to be part of that plan now.

Downstairs, my curiosity gets the best of me. The kitchen table's covered in sketches and scribbles and I grin at how messy it is. I pick up one of the drawings—an outline of a bar logo with the name "Priestly's" woven into the design. My throat tightens as I trace my finger over my last name—*our* last name—incorporated into her dream.

I'm still looking at the designs when I hear Clover's footsteps on the stairs. She pauses in the doorway, our son no longer in her arms.

"He's out," she says, moving to join me at the table. "Hopefully for more than forty-five minutes this time."

I hold up the sketch. "You're naming the bar after us?"

She nods, leaning into me as my arm automatically wraps around her waist. "It seemed right." She repeats my own words back to me from the day I put the mobile up in our son's room.

"Starting your empire, Freckles?" I murmur against her hair, inhaling the citrus scent of her shampoo mixed with the baby smell that seems to cling to both of us these days.

"Somebody has to plan for the future in this relationship," she teases, but there's a softness to her voice that wasn't there before all of this started. Something just for me. "You like it?"

"I do," I tell her, and I mean it.

She turns in my arms, her hands sliding up my chest as she looks up at me. Even though we're both running on no sleep and covered in baby spit, she's never looked happier.

A small noise comes from the baby monitor on the counter. We both freeze, holding our breath until it's clear he's not waking up.

Clover laughs under her breath. "We're gonna do that for at least the next eighteen years, aren't we?"

"At minimum, since he's the oldest." She protests a little at that as I tug her closer, resting my chin on the top of her head. "We're in this for the long haul, Freckles."

"I'm gonna need a solid eight hours of sleep before we even start to think about another one." She rises on her tiptoes, her lips brushing mine in a gentle kiss that still packs the power to set my blood on fire. One hand skims my jaw, the other slipping around my waist as I cup her face, taking in the warmth of her skin.

When we break apart, her eyes meet mine, that electric blue crackling with the same spark that got me hooked in the first place. It hasn't faded. Not with time, not with pregnancy, not with sleepless nights and dirty diapers and the million little challenges that come with building a life together.

It's in that moment, standing in our kitchen with my wife in my arms and our son sleeping upstairs, that I realize what I've been fighting fires for all these years. Not just to save others, but to deserve to come home to this. To them. To the family I never thought I'd have, the love I never saw coming and now can't live without.

I press my wife back against the kitchen counter, claiming her mouth in a kiss that promises we're just getting started. Ever after suddenly feels too short for everything I want with this woman.

She smiles into the kiss. "I love you, Banks Priestly," she whispers.

"I love you too, Clover Priestly," I reply, voice rough. "For fucking ever."

Her smile—that one that's just for me—lights up my entire world. "For fucking ever," she agrees.

And in that moment, even after thirty-six sleepless hours, even with the hardest job in the world waiting for us upstairs, I know with absolute certainty that I'm exactly where I'm meant to be. That everything in my life—every fire, every risk, every twist and turn—was leading me here.

Home.

WANT *more?*

Want to know what happened between Kasen & Banks outside of the brewery?

Read the FREE bonus scene here:

heatherashley.myflodesk.com/ueabonus1

Clover's PLANT INDEX

Mint Julep (Julie) – The cherished firstborn. This thriving mint plant has survived a move and a spider mite infestation. Resilient and demanding, Julie needs morning sun and plenty of attention, but rewards Clover with steady growth and reliability. The favorite child.

Manhattan – The original companion. This ivy plant has been with Clover since her first lonely week of college, turning a sterile dorm room into something that felt like home. The quiet, dependable friend who's seen Clover through every transformation.

Mojito – The confidante. This sword fern on the bedroom windowsill has heard every secret, every fear, and every late-night crisis. Elegant but sturdy, Mojito doesn't judge, just listens while Clover works through her problems.

Moscow Mule – Banks's favorite and the neediest of the bunch. This struggling Monstera requires constant reassurance and care. High-maintenance but worth the effort.

Bellini – The bathroom dweller. This jade plant thrives in steam and humidity, witnessing Clover's most vulnerable moments. Sturdy and unshakable, Bellini's seen it all and keeps those secrets safe.

Mai Tai – The wanderer. This floor-dwelling Pothos gets moved around the apartment to chase the best light. Adaptable and easygoing, Mai Tai makes the best of any situation – the perfect plant for someone learning to go with the flow.

Old Fashioned – The introvert. Unlike the sun-lovers, this moody plant prefers shadows and indirect light. Mysterious and a bit dramatic, Old Fashioned proves that sometimes the ones requiring special handling are worth the extra effort.

White Russian – The survivor. Despite Clover's occasional neglect, White Russian persists through drought and darkness. Stubbornly determined to live, much like its owner, this plant refuses to give up even when conditions aren't ideal.

a letter from the author

(If you want to avoid politics, this is your warning to skip this note)

HI, friend!

I don't think it's a secret I've been struggling to write my dark stuff for a while now. I thought it was just writer's block, but it turns out that the state of the world (okay, the U.S.) has really been impacting my mental health and I needed a break from the dark.

It's hard to want to write over the top men who take what they want without asking for permission when you see women's rights being trampled on and taken away every day. It's a serious struggle for me.

So I thought I'd just have some fun with this one. There's not a lot of angst (well, unless you count wanting to punch Clover in the boob for being such a dumbass in chapter 11) and it really just let me have all sorts of dopamine hits and good feels as I was writing it.

I know a lot of people hate the pregnancy trope and babies in books of any kind because this is their escape, but I love how it brings my characters together on a deeper level. There's just something about that for me that hits different in MF romance.

I will say, the prospect of getting pregnant again IRL gives me legit panic attacks so getting to have fun with it here is the perfect outlet for me. I hope babies and men who are feral for them give you all the warm fuzzies like they do me.

And hey, if not at least making 'em is fun.

Anyway, things suck right now and as you've likely already guessed based on that chapter 23, Kasen's book is up next because my heart (and, more importantly, creativity!) is with this series at the moment.

So get ready for some enemies-to-lovers, grumpy/sunshine fun in book 2, Reluctantly Ever After.

Until then...

Wishing you good things and due process,

Heather

find me

- [Instagram] @heatherashleywrites
- [Threads] @heatherashleyauthor
- [Facebook] /heatherashleywrites
- [Pinterest] /heatherwritesitall
- [Bluesky] @heatherashley.bsky.social
- [Patreon] /heatherashleywrites

heatherashleywrites.com

About the Author

Heather Ashley writes dark & steamy forbidden stories with toxic, obsessive heroes. She's a PNW girl through and through and lives for foggy mornings among the evergreens.

Printed in Great Britain
by Amazon